FALLING GRACEFULLY

A LESBIAN ROMANCE

CARA MALONE

CHAPTER ONE

MELODY

The cramped lobby of Mary Beth's School of Dance was packed with young ballerinas and their parents when Melody Bledsoe walked in. She was holding a newspaper in her hand, folded to the classified section with a big red circle traced around an ad. It seemed like a terribly archaic way to find a job, but Melody's mother laid the newspaper in front of her this morning along with her breakfast, and Melody knew she had to at least ask for an application.

The job was for a front desk receptionist, and by the utter chaos happening here, it was clear that Mary Beth needed to fill this position desperately. The waiting area was only about ten feet square, and in that space there were at least eight adults and, well, Melody gave up trying to count the kids because they all pinballed around the room in constant motion. Most of the girls were wearing pink leotards and ballet skirts, a few colorful tutus took up even more of the tight space, and they were all waiting for class to begin.

Melody couldn't have chosen a more chaotic time to arrive.

When she finally made her way to the desk, weaving past a dozen parents all trying to wrangle their kids into ballet slippers, the woman behind the counter looked just as frayed as Melody's nerves felt. Her wispy gray hair stuck out of her bun in a dozen odd angles and she was frantically trying to do three things at once.

"Who's here for the one p.m. beginner ballet class?" She asked, her large voice booming into the room above the ruckus. "Don't forget to sign in on the clipboard before you go into the room. Anyone need to make a payment? Who's here to pick up their costume for the recital? Dressing room is down the hall - please try on your costume before you leave. The time to make alterations is running out!"

Melody watched wide-eyed as the diminutive woman rattled all these things off, moving from task to task and knocking things over as she tried to move behind the small reception desk and was thwarted at every turn by a mound of costumes in plastic bags, parents clambering for the sign-in sheet, and kids running underfoot.

It was dizzying, and Melody was just about to elbow her way back out of the room when the woman barked, "Whatcha need, kiddo?"

It took a moment before Melody realized that the woman was talking to her, and then she felt tongue-tied. What did she need in this anarchy?

"Umm, you're hiring?" Melody said meekly, her voice barely audible above the commotion in the room. She lifted the newspaper and pointed to the ad.

"Oh, great!" The woman exclaimed. "You've got good timing. As you can see, I could use all the help I can get, especially with this recital coming up fast. Would you mind stepping behind the desk for a few minutes? I gotta pee like a racehorse."

"Uh-" Melody started to object, but the woman was already squeezing out from behind the desk.

"Consider it a working interview," she called as she headed down the hall at one end of the lobby. Then she added with a laugh, "Or a trial by fire, if you prefer. You don't have to do anything - just get people to sign in if they're here for ballet and if they need anything else, tell them Mary Beth will be back in a few minutes."

"But-"

"Thank you!" the woman called, and then she darted into a small bathroom halfway down the hall and slammed the door.

"Oh boy," Melody muttered under her breath.

If this was how Mary Beth's School of Dance functioned, she wasn't sure her nerves could handle a job here. She thought about heading for the door – she could be halfway back to her parents' house before Mary Beth even flushed the toilet – but then a velvety voice behind her asked, "Is this where we're supposed to be?"

"I was just wondering the exact same thing," Melody said, turning to find the owner of the voice. It turned out to be a stunningly pretty woman with pin-straight, carrot-red hair and vibrant green eyes. Her teeth grazed briefly across her lower lip as their eyes locked, and then she looked away, squeezing the hand of a little girl in a black leotard.

"I'm looking for the beginner ballet class," the woman said. "I spoke to Mary Beth on the phone and she said we could try the first class for free since it's the end of the year."

Melody couldn't stop staring into those mossy green eyes. She thought the woman didn't look nearly old enough to have a kid that age.

"Yeah," she found herself saying, "the clipboard's right here."

CHAPTER TWO

JESSIE

J essie Cartwright hadn't been on time for anything but work in the last five years, and judging by the scene that greeted her at Mary Beth's, her daughter wasn't off to a much better start.

Ellie had been begging to take ballet lessons ever since they watched The Nutcracker on TV a few months ago, and when Jessie figured out that she could try it out for the price of a pair of ballet slippers and a leotard, she was determined to make it work around her schedule. If Ellie liked the class, it would mean extra shifts at the grocery store to cover the cost of lessons, but it was worth it to Jessie if it made Ellie happy. That was her philosophy.

Today they had to rush across town, Jessie's speedometer dancing just over the speed limit, in order to get here on time but they made it just as a dozen little ballerinas and their mothers started filing into the dance studio.

Class was starting and Jessie still had to sign Ellie in and figure out why her ballet slippers kept falling off on the car ride over here.

"Hurry, bug," Jessie cooed as she pulled Ellie along. That might as well have been the anthem to their lives, rushing the poor kid from place to place while Jessie tried to make it seem like she had everything under control. In reality, she *never* knew what the hell she was doing. She wasn't sure if that was the plight of the teen mother, or *all* mothers.

There was no one behind the reception desk and Jessie wanted to throw her hands up in exasperation – she probably hadn't taken a full breath since she dashed out of the store to go collect Ellie from her mother's house twenty minutes ago. Thankfully, a girl standing in front of the counter heard her frustration and stepped in to help.

"I think you just need to sign your name in the column for beginner ballet," she said as she passed Jessie the clipboard and a pen from the desk.

"Thanks," Jessie said breathlessly, dropping Ellie's hand to sign her in.

As she took the clipboard out of the girl's hand, their eyes locked in a more substantial way than Jessie was expecting. The girl had large, chestnut-colored eyes and for some reason Jessie couldn't explain, they had the effect of clearing all the chaos out of the room. She didn't hear little feet running across the hardwood in the studio anymore, and she didn't feel all the people moving around her in the lobby. She was locked into this girl's gaze and for a moment, nothing else existed.

Jessie caught herself after a second and looked down at the clipboard, saying, "Umm, my name or my daughter's name?"

"Let's see," the girl said, leaning over the clipboard and scanning the list of names already written on the sign-in sheet. She smelled like peppermint and she said with a wry smile, "I don't know many dance moms named Zenith, so I think it's supposed to be her name, not yours."

Jessie laughed, acutely aware of the narrow space between her and the girl. She was tall and lean, with nearly black hair and dark features that continued to draw Jessie in. But of course she was standing close to Jessie – she suddenly remembered that the lobby had about a thousand people in it, even if they had all vanished in the moment she looked into the girl's eyes. She forced her own eyes back down to the sign-in sheet and she wrote *Elizabeth Cartwright.*

"Oh thank god," the girl said with an exaggerated sigh. "I thought for sure you were going to write Sony or Panasonic and then I'd be in trouble."

"Her middle name's Toshiba if that makes you feel any better," Jessie said, and Ellie smacked her thigh before she got to fully enjoy the smile spreading across the girl's lips.

"No it isn't, it's Mae," she corrected. "Come on, mommy, they're all going in."

She was right – the lobby was clearing out as

everyone filed into the studio, leaving Jessie and Ellie and the girl with the chestnut eyes.

"Okay, girls!" Someone suddenly called out in a booming voice that Jessie recognized from the phone. Mary Beth herself was coming down the hall, ready to begin the lesson. "Everyone into the studio, it's time to warm up!"

She rushed past the reception desk, throwing a quick wink at Jessie – or maybe it was directed at the girl, she couldn't tell – and then disappeared into the studio.

"Come *on*," Ellie said again, tugging at Jessie's hand. "They're starting!"

"Okay, okay, bug," Jessie said. She handed the clipboard to the girl and forced herself to come back to reality. What the hell had come over her, anyway? She turned to Ellie. "We still have to figure out how to get your shoes to stay on your feet. Sit in that chair and we'll give it one more try."

She pointed to a chair on the wall next to the reception desk and pulled a small pair of ballet slippers out of her back pocket, kneeling down to try and put them on again. Ellie was looking over Jessie's shoulder at the kids stretching on the floor, and she was so eager to join them that she barely held still long enough for Jessie to catch her foot and shove one of the slippers over it. She was swinging her legs and bouncing in the seat, and Jessie wanted to get her into that room as much as Ellie did – if she burned off some of that raw energy, maybe Jessie could squeeze in a rare nap this afternoon – but the damn shoes kept popping off every time Ellie wiggled her toes.

"Sit still or you're never gonna get to dance," Jessie warned, catching Ellie's swinging foot again as she muttered to herself, "I don't understand. Are these things defective?"

"Did they come with elastics?"

"Huh?"

The girl had been watching Jessie's struggle and she asked again, "When you bought them, did they come with a pair of elastics?"

"Oh," Jessie said, "Maybe. I just bought them before we came."

"Oh," the girl said with a laugh. "Well, I hope you kept the box because the elastics are kinda necessary."

"Figures," Jessie said. She was kicking herself for not planning all this better – it didn't even occur to her that Ellie needed shoes to try out a free class until her mother mentioned it this morning, but who knew ballet slippers required assembly, anyway?

Jessie's train of thought was interrupted as she realized the girl was crouching down beside her. Again she could smell peppermint on her breath and Jessie felt flushed for no reason. The girl wasn't paying attention to Jessie, though. She turned to her daughter instead and asked, "Elizabeth, right?"

"Ellie."

"Ellie, do you mind if I take a look at your shoes?"

"No," she said, and just like that all of the squirm and excess energy went out of her. She always was good about minding her manners for strangers, and she held out her feet obediently.

The girl removed the slipper that was dangling precariously from Ellie's toes, and Jessie handed over the other one. Her fingers brushed across the girl's palm for a split second and a light shiver ran through her. Jessie convinced herself that it was nothing more than a gust of air blowing under the door that made her react like that, because if it wasn't cold air then she didn't know what had gotten into her.

"Unfortunately, there's nothing we can do about these right now," the girl said to Ellie after examining the slippers. "No matter how tight we pull the string, you're just going to keep dancing right out of your shoes without those elastics. I bet Mary Beth would let you dance in your tights just this once if you tell her it's your first lesson."

"Sorry, bug," Jessie said. "Mommy screwed up."

"It's okay," Ellie said. "Can I go in now?"

"Yeah," Jessie answered, "Go ahead, I'll be right behind you. Be careful – don't slip and fall in those tights!"

Ellie burst out of the chair, darting between Jessie and the girl and nearly setting them both off balance as she bolted into the studio.

"Hi, I'm Ellie," Jessie could hear her saying to the other kids, and Jessie smiled, letting herself rock backward to sit on the floor a moment. Ellie made it to class and Jessie could finally catch her breath.

"That was dumb of me," she said to the girl, who was still crouching beside her. Juggling two jobs, a kid, and the sleep deprivation that came along with it all did a number on her common sense sometimes and she said with an apologetic shrug, "The box is in my car so the elastics must be in it."

"No worries," the girl said with that megawatt smile. "When you get home, sew them in with a needle and thread – they come separate so you can fit them specially to Ellie's feet. Put the slippers on her and tighten the string, then line the elastics up with her arches. I usually pin mine in place, take the slippers off, and then sew them in."

"Thanks," Jessie said. "You've been really helpful."

"You wanna hear something funny?" the girl asked.

"What?"

"I don't even work here," she said with a laugh. "I came to apply for the receptionist job and got thrown into something called a 'working interview,' which Mary Beth may or may not have forgotten about already. You want to be my reference?"

Jessie laughed and said, "Sure. I'm Jessie, by the way."

She extended her hand to the girl and felt her stomach trying to climb into her throat. She hadn't felt giddy like this since high school and she nearly yanked her hand away, but it was too late and the girl's fingers slid into hers.

Jessie's heart skipped a beat, and she told herself to stop being ridiculous.

The girl introduced herself as Melody and Jessie liked watching her mouth form the word. Her lips were so pink and her tongue tapped against her teeth on the *lo* syllable, and Jessie had the sudden urge to try the name out in her own mouth.

"So, Melody," she said, blushing slightly and then soldiering on, "You must be a dancer if you know this much about ballet slippers and you don't even work here."

"Nope, just a savant who wandered in off the street," Melody said, cracking a smile to let Jessie know it was a joke. Her eyes lit up and Jessie could see little flecks of gold in them. Then her smile broke into a smirk and she said, "I used to be a dancer. Not anymore, though."

"What hap-"

"*Mommy!*" Jessie heard Ellie shriek from the studio and she instantly went pink in the cheeks. So much for those good manners. Ellie called, "Where are you?"

It was a blessing and a curse to have such an extroverted child, and someday soon Jessie would have to go over the rules of ballet etiquette with her – including the fact that it was not polite to screech in the middle of a lesson, especially while classical music was playing serenely in the background.

For now, though, Jessie really ought to get in there. She got up from the floor and dusted glitter from her pants – the whole lobby seemed to be covered in a fine layer of the stuff from the pile of costumes behind the reception desk – then she said, "It was nice meeting you, Melody. Thanks again for your help."

"No problem," Melody said, standing up beside her. "I hope Ellie enjoys the class."

Jessie gave one more backward glance at Melody

before she stepped into the studio. There was a row of folding chairs along one wall and that's where all the other moms were sitting, each one of them holding a note-book in her hands and diligently taking notes about everything Mary Beth did with the dancers. Jessie found a seat and smiled at Ellie, who was doing her best to keep up with them despite the fact that they had an entire year's jump on her.

Her mind kept going back to Melody, though. There was something about her that Jessie couldn't shake – something magnetic, and she sensed it could be dangerous if she didn't shut down this feeling right away.

CHAPTER THREE

MELODY

Melody took a seat behind the front desk after Jessie disappeared into the studio. It seemed silly to leave now, after all the work was done and before she had a chance to talk to Mary Beth about the receptionist job. Melody was pretty certain she had it in the bag if she wanted it, but that was another reason to get up and walk out right now.

She could go home and tell her mother that she tried and it wouldn't really be a lie. She'd never have to know that Melody left before Mary Beth finalized her so-called working interview.

Melody sighed and looked at the mess surrounding the desk. There was a giant mound of sequined and glittering costumes to her left and a few weeks' worth of sign-in sheets scattered across the desk. Mary Beth really did need help, but Melody wasn't sure how much more dance she could handle in her life. Even if she wasn't dealing directly with the students here, being the

14

receptionist still might be too much for her to handle right now. Why couldn't her mother have found her an ad for a waitress, or a deli clerk, or a telemarketer instead?

She glanced at the clock on the wall in front of her and saw that it was only fifteen after one. Classes like this usually ran for an hour, but she might as well stick around since she'd come this far. She turned to the pile of costumes and started going through them, straightening them out and organizing them according to the names scribbled on the plastic garment bags.

FORTY-FIVE MINUTES LATER, the studio door opened just as Melody predicted and the class let out. She waved goodbye to Ellie as she came tearing out of the studio, thrilled with her first ballet lesson, and Jessie's eyes lingered on Melody's from across the crowded lobby.

Then they were gone and Mary Beth was finally making her way back to the desk.

"How are you doing, kiddo?" she asked.

"Fine I guess," Melody said. "I organized the costumes alphabetically. I hope that's okay."

"Okay?" Mary Beth asked, a wide grin spreading over her face. "I'd kiss you if you weren't my employee. You're in, right?"

"Yeah," Melody said, despite the fact that she'd never felt more uncertain about a decision in her life. Had the gorgeous redhead really had that big an impact on her that she was willing to put herself through dance studio hell just to see her again?

"Great," Mary Beth said. "We've been in dire need for someone with your organizing skills, and they'll come in handy during the recital next month."

"I have to go to that?" Melody asked, blanching at the thought of being surrounded by all those costumes, not to mention the stage lights and the auditorium. She really didn't know what she'd gotten herself into.

"Yeah, I need somebody to keep the dancers organized and make sure they get to the stage on time," Mary Beth said. "Don't worry, it's not hard and the whole thing's over in a couple of hours."

She didn't give Melody any further chance to object before she was moving on and talking about the studio's schedule and Melody's shifts at the reception desk. It was clear that Mary Beth had a lot of enthusiasm but she didn't run the tightest ship around. Melody tried not to pay any attention to the racing of her heart and pushed thoughts of the recital out of her head as she accepted the job, telling herself it would be fine and she'd cross that bridge when she came to it. If worse came to worst, she could always quit.

"Is that going to be a problem?"

"What?" Melody asked, realizing that she missed the last bit of Mary Beth's words while she was imagining herself backstage.

"I was saying that the studio closes down for a couple months every summer right after the recital," Mary Beth said, not the least bit annoyed at having to repeat herself.

She probably got that from being surrounded by hyper kids all day. "I know it's not the best situation to be hired and then immediately have to take the summer off, but I really need help during the recital so is that going to be okay with you?"

"Oh," Melody said. "Yeah, that's fine."

If the recital turned out anything like the last time Melody came near a stage, she might need that time to recover.

"Good to hear, kiddo," Mary Beth said, extending her hand. "Welcome aboard."

TWENTY MINUTES LATER, after Mary Beth gave Melody a perfunctory training session on running the desk and then handed her a class schedule to coincide with Melody's new work hours, she walked outside having landed her very first job. Her mother would be thrilled.

The cool spring air filled her lungs and Melody still hadn't quite gotten Jessie out of her mind. She was a gorgeous girl with an intriguing stoicism running like a current behind her moss-colored eyes, and a small part of Melody hoped to find her lingering out here. Of course, that wasn't realistic and the parking lot was nearly empty, so she started the trek back to her neighborhood six blocks away.

It was a nice afternoon. Sweater weather mixed with the fresh smell of new life as everything turned green and flowers were in bloom. Instead of going straight home, though, Melody took a familiar detour. She cut across the tall grass of a yard three houses down from her parents' place and let herself into a door on the side of the house without knocking. She went down a flight of creaky stairs to a cool, partially finished basement that she'd gotten to know quite well in the past six months.

"Andy?" She called as she reached the bottom of the stairs. "You home?"

The basement was one large room with cinderblock walls and concrete floors, and aside from the washer and dryer in one corner and the furnace in another, it looked like a stoner kid's studio apartment. There was a mattress along one wall with its box springs sitting directly on the concrete and a makeshift living room in the center of the open space.

The stoner kid himself, Andy, was sitting on the couch playing some shoot-em-up video game and spooning soggy cereal into his mouth from a bowl cradled in his crotch.

"Hey," he said without looking at her, his eyes locked on the television.

"Did you just get up?" Melody asked incredulously as she flopped into the reclining chair beside the couch that she'd come to think of as hers.

"So what if I did?" Andy asked around a mouthful of cereal, pausing the game.

"It's almost three," Melody said.

"Okay, little miss judgmental," Andy said, "What have *you* done today that's so impressive?"

"Well, I guess that depends on your definition of impressive," she said, glancing at a rather large bong sitting on the coffee table in front of them, then she added, "but I did get a job."

"No shit," Andy said, drinking his cereal milk and putting the bowl on the table. He picked up the bong and said, "Does this mean the golden child is finally back on her feet?"

"Hardly," Melody said. "It's a part-time gig with almost zero responsibility. Not exactly what you'd expect a golden child to be doing with her life."

"What *is* the golden doing with her life?" Andy asked, digging a lighter out from between the cushions of the couch. "Aside from hanging out in my basement and making disparaging remarks about my lifestyle?"

"About the same as you," she said. "Except with less stains on my clothes."

"Ouch," Andy said as he grabbed the lighter and put it to the bong. With his lips hovering just above the glass, he said, "Seriously, what's the gig?"

"Receptionist at a dance studio," Melody said quickly, trying to distract them both from this admission by getting off the recliner with a grunt and going over to a mini fridge beside the television.

Andy didn't object when she made herself at home, retrieving a pair of sodas before plopping back down in the recliner, but he did snort at her new job, coughing as the air filled with an opaque cloud. Melody tossed one of the sodas on the couch beside him, gently enough that it wouldn't explode when he opened it, and then waited while he recovered.

"You're joking, right?"

"Nope," Melody said, offering no further explanation as she took a sip of her soda.

"That's the last place I thought you'd want to work," Andy said. He didn't know much about why she came home from New York after only four months there, but he knew it was all about ballet and her brief enrollment in the Pavlova School.

"Right you are," Melody said. "Tell him what he's won, Johnny!"

Ignoring this quip, Andy asked, "So what gives?"

"My parents," Melody said with another roll of her eyes. "And what they gave was an ultimatum. There's something about having a really promising career ahead of you and dashing it against the rocks that tends to make parents kinda grumpy."

"I don't understand them," Andy said with a shrug and a glance toward the ceiling, in reference to his own parents. "You'd think they would be thrilled that we're helping them ward off Empty Nest Syndrome by staying as long as possible."

Melody and Andy lived a few doors down from each other their whole lives, but she never really knew him until she came home from New York City six months ago with her head hung low. When they were kids, he was a boy and she was a girl, and when they reached puberty and started looking at everyone differently, well, he was a boy and she was into girls. More important to Melody's parents, though, he was a stoner with no ambitions who spent all of his time in his parents' basement. That was not the type of friend the Bledsoes wanted for their darling daughter, who was driven and talented and destined for great things.

When she came back to her hometown of Lisbon, though, Melody found that suddenly she was a loser with no ambitions who didn't mind the idea of spending all her time in a basement, too. And so, a new friendship predicated on apathy was born.

"They've got my sister for that," Melody said. "Besides, I think they were looking forward to turning my bedroom into an office."

"So are they making you pay rent or something?" Andy asked. "My mom tried that right after I graduated but I was able to bargain her down to yard work."

"The yard looks like shit," Melody said and Andy laughed and took another rip off the bong. She waited until he set it on the coffee table, motioning it away politely when he offered it to her, and then she leaned back into the old recliner before adding, "My dad's been on my case for months to stop 'wallowing around the house' and figure out what I'm going to do with my life. I don't think he'll be appeased if I mow the lawn every now and then. He keeps saying 'six months is long enough to get over anything'."

"What *are* you getting over?" Andy asked. Melody shot him a withering glare and he put his hands up. "Hey, it was worth a shot. You're never going to tell me what happened in New York, are you?"

"Nope," Melody said. "I would never tell anyone if I had my way. My parents only know because they're the ones that had to drive out there and pick me up, and I had to tell Doctor Riley because otherwise what would we talk about for an hour every week? Besides the three of them, though, I'm planning to take it to my grave."

"Okay, okay," Andy said. "And yet you're going to work in a dance studio. Why not be a waitress, or a quirky indie bookshop girl, or a dog groomer?"

"Are those the kinds of jobs you see me doing?"

"Maybe if you dye your hair hot pink," Andy said with a shrug.

"Well, I spent three months appeasing my dad by applying for every job I could find online, and the only thing I found was that no one wants high school grads with no practical experience," Melody said. "My mom found the dance studio job, and I'm not really in a position to turn it away. She thinks it'll help – as if it's exposure therapy or something. I told her Dr. Riley never approved that, but she was persistent."

"You'll be fine," Andy said with a shrug. "It's just a desk job."

That was exactly the kind of flippant attitude Melody's parents had when it came to getting a job – it hadn't even occurred to her mother that the mere thought of stepping foot in a dance studio was enough to send Melody into a panic attack. No one understood – how could they? – and that was exactly why Melody would never tell Andy or anyone else but her therapist about the events leading up to her New York disgrace last winter.

After a long silence, Melody said, "At least there's one up side to working at Mary Beth's."

"What's that?"

"The dance moms." Melody blushed and looked down at the grungy carpet, suddenly embarrassed at her own words.

Andy guffawed and clapped his hands together, asking with a wide smile, "Melody Bledsoe, are you into cougars?"

She already wished she could take back her comment. It was a mistake.

"Not really," she said.

"But there's one particular cougar who caught your eye," Andy guessed. "Is it Mary Beth?"

"Gross, she's more like a saber-toothed tiger," Melody said, unable to keep from smirking.

Mary Beth with her silver hair and loud mouth would never be Melody's type. Jessie, on the other hand... she'd been running through Melody's mind ever since she left the school, and it felt like she might burst if she didn't tell someone about their encounter. There were sparks... weren't there?

"This girl's not really a cougar," she said. "She looks young, like she had kids early. Her daughter's around five, so I'd guess she's about twenty-three? No older than that for sure."

"You're okay with the kid?" Andy asked. "Or do you just want to bang her?"

"That's so crude," Melody chastised. "Unlike you, I don't immediately want to screw everyone I meet."

"Sure," Andy said. "When's the U-Haul coming?"

"That is such a played-out stereotype," Melody said, glaring at him. "At least be original with your lesbian jokes."

"I can't help it," Andy said with another shrug. "You're the only one I know. So is she gay or do you think I have a better shot with her?"

"You don't have a shot with her regardless of her orientation," Melody said with a laugh.

She had not attempted to flirt with a girl since... well, now that she was thinking about it, Melody wasn't sure if she'd ever actually flirted with someone. Sure, there had been crushes in high school, and a meaningless kiss here and there. But for as long as Melody could remember, there had also been ballet. Ballet practice, ballet rehearsal, ballet recital, ballet auditions. Ballet before school, and after school, and in her sleep. It always came first and there was never time for anything else.

Now, though, Melody found herself with an abundance of time. There was time to figure out what her life should be about now that ballet was off the table, and time to explore the world beyond her pointe shoes.

So why the hell was she working at a ballet studio and crushing on the dance moms there?

"I probably won't pursue it," she said with a shrug.

"Why not?" Andy asked, getting irritated with her because living vicariously through Melody was one of the only ways that he ever left the basement.

"I don't know," Melody said. "It seems dumb to... mix business with pleasure?"

"You're scared," Andy said, leaving her no room to argue.

"Whatever," Melody said, checking the clock on her phone. "I gotta go home."

It was nearly dinner time and her parents would expect her to come home with a report about how the job application went. She heaved herself up from the depths of the recliner and gave herself a quick spritz with the can of Febreze that Andy kept on the coffee table. It wasn't a perfect solution, or an elegant one, but she was always nervous that the skunky smell of weed clung to her clothes when she left the basement, and this would at least mask the worst of it.

Melody went the first eighteen years of her life without having tried so much as a can of beer or a cigarette. That was another area of her life in which ballet trumped all the normal teenage interests, but now there was no reason to worry about drug tests or hangovers or decreased lung capacity. Andy passed her the bong on the first night that she came down to the basement after she came back to Lisbon, and after he got done dying of laughter when she looked at him with eyes wide and asked him what was in it, she took her first hit of weed.

It was okay – nothing special – and it made her tired, so most of the time she just hung out in the basement and let Andy have all the fun. That didn't mean Melody wanted to go through the hassle of letting her parents think she was throwing her life away even more than she already had by coming home reeking of marijuana. It certainly wouldn't endear Andy to them, who Melody's father once called a mooching deadbeat. That was before Melody moved home and became a mooching deadbeat herself, so she could only imagine the high opinion of Andy that they must hold now that he was her best friend.

Melody took the stairs two at a time while Andy flopped back on the couch and turned his attention back to the television.

CHAPTER FOUR

MELODY

"No," Melody said, "They haven't posted the list yet."

She held her phone between her shoulder and her ear and was trying to balance on a narrow bench in the locker room. There were a dozen other girls buzzing around her, changing into leotards and tights and chattering at each other, and it was hard to hear over the commotion.

"But how do you think you did?" Her mother was asking. "Good enough to get out of the chorus this time?"

"I don't know, mom," Melody said, an edge of irritation coming into her voice despite her best efforts to bite it back.

She had five minutes to put her hair in a bun, jam her sore feet into her pointe shoes, and warm up before class began, and her mother had a way of choosing the most inopportune times to badger her. Melody had been at Pavlova for three months and after every single try-out, her mother pestered her relentlessly for the results.

"*Please don't take that tone with me,*" her mother said, and Melody shut her eyes, feeling a tension headache coming on. Once it started, the only way to treat it was with a big, juicy chicken breast, or something else loaded with protein. Too bad for her, she still had two more hours of class before she could stop to eat something. Her mother was still talking when she zoned back into the conversation, struggling with her pointe shoe at the same time. "... forty thousand dollars a year. Your father and I had to make a lot of sacrifices for you to go-"

"*It's not like I'm volunteering for the choral spots,*" Melody snapped as she pulled a thick lambs' wool pad over her blistered toes and pain screamed up her leg. "I gotta go, mom. I'll call you tonight."

She pulled the lambs' wool off her toes and tossed her phone angrily into her duffel bag. There were bandages wrapped around almost every one of her toes, raw and bloodied where her knuckles scraped against the insides of her pointe shoes day in and day out. Even on the weekends when she didn't have class, Melody put in three or four hours in the practice studio, and her poor, battered feet never got a break.

That was the price of being a Pavlova ballerina, though, and every one of the other girls rushing around the locker room had pulled her shoes on over blistered, bloodied toes without complaining about it. Melody set her jaw and prepared to do the same.

It really only hurt while she was getting into her shoes. Adrenaline had a wonderful way of taking away the pain once she was on the dance floor. That was when she could *feel the music flowing through her body and see the stage whenever she closed her eyes. Those were the moments when all this pain and trouble was worth it, and when she could forget about the fact that she'd been put in the chorus for every one of the performances she auditioned for since she arrived.*

In the space between blinks, she was a prima ballerina.

CHAPTER FIVE

JESSIE

T he world outside of Jessie's window was pitch black except for the yellow glow of a street light when she finally got to slouch into her favorite over-stuffed old chair. Like most of the things in their half of the little duplex, the chair was a hand-me-down from her parents and about five years past its prime. It was still plenty comfortable to curl up in during the rare moments when Jessie had a chance to relax.

This wasn't one of those moments, but at least she could bring her work with her. Pulling a little side table next to the chair, she set her sewing kit on top of it along with the elastics for Ellie's ballet slippers. Jessie wasn't the best seamstress in the world, but she could sew a button and darn a sock, and she bet that she could figure this out, too.

Ellie had ricocheted all around the house after her ballet lesson ended, showing Jessie first position, second position, plié and arabesque over and over again. She was quite pleased with herself, refusing to change out of her leotard even for dinner. Jessie watched her swinging her feet beneath the table, turning them out and pushing her heels together into first position as she shoved chicken nuggets and macaroni into her mouth. There was no doubt she'd be signing Ellie up for lessons in the fall.

"Mary Beth said there's a recital next month," Ellie said, little flecks of chicken flying across the table.

"Chew first, talk after you swallow," Jessie scolded, trying to look severe. It was hard to maintain the expression, though, because she couldn't help swelling with pride at how excited Ellie was about ballet. All of those extra hours she'd have to put in at work would be worth it if she could see the joy they paid for.

"They're going to dance on a stage and wear costumes and everything," Ellie continued. "I don't know the dance but Mary Beth says I should come anyway and watch so I know what it'll be like when I get to dance next year."

After dinner, Jessie tucked the elastics into Ellie's ballet slippers the way Melody told her to, pinning them in place and then carefully removing the slippers to keep from sticking her feet with the straight pins. Jessie didn't have a quiet moment to actually finish the job until after Ellie went to bed, sleeping more soundly than she had since she was a baby. Jessie thought she'd probably used up all her energy for the entire week today, but of course Ellie would wake up tomorrow ready to go again.

For now, though, she took advantage of the quiet moment to sew in Ellie's elastics.

The house was silent as she worked – Jessie hadn't watched much television in the last five years and she didn't have much use for it. Even if she had the time to get invested in a show, it seemed like every one of them was nothing but a love story. Even if it was a thriller, or a crime drama, or a reality show, there had to be a love story. They were inescapable and tiring. So when she had a rare moment to herself, Jessie learned to enjoy the sound of silence.

Jessie was just picking up the second ballet slipper when she heard a key slide into the front door. She looked up from her work and her husband came into the living room.

"Hey, Jess," Steve said, nodding briefly at her before turning his back and unzipping his coveralls. As always, they were smeared with grease from the machines he worked with, and after a few hours of hard scrubbing to get it out of the carpet when he first took the job, Jessie gave him strict orders to leave them by the door to save her the mess.

"Hi," she said as he kicked off his work boots. "How was your day?"

"It was alright," Steve said with his characteristic shrug. His hair could have caught on fire, or he could have played the lottery and won a million dollars during his dinner hour and he still would have answered with *it was alright* and a shrug. "How about you?"

"Good," Jessie said. "Ellie enjoyed her ballet lesson."

"Oh, that was today? Good," Steve answered. "Is she asleep?"

"Mm hmm," Jessie said, not even bothering to look at him as she answered. She kept her eyes on the tiny ballet slipper in her hands, careful not to poke herself with the needle as she threaded it through the elastic.

Steve always got home from work a little past nine and Ellie went to bed at eight-thirty, and yet he asked that question every night. He'd go into her room in a couple of minutes and kiss her goodnight, and most of the time she didn't even stir.

"There's mac and cheese in the fridge," Jessie said.

"Thanks," Steve answered. "What time are you working tomorrow?"

"Grocery store from seven to two, then waitressing til eight," Jessie said, although she had to pause a minute to think about it. Two jobs had been manageable when she used to work only one of them each day, picking up shifts at the diner on the weekends for extra money, but now that she was waitressing more frequently in order to bank money for Ellie's dance lessons, it was harder to keep her schedule straight. "You?"

"The usual," Steve said. "Twelve to nine."

He carefully stepped out of the coveralls and hung them on a coat rack, and then he was wearing just a pair of boxers and an old yellowed tee shirt – he spent six days a week in coveralls at the factory, and aside from taking Ellie to school in the mornings, he had no need for anything but the coveralls. Jessie watched him meandering toward the kitchen and noted with mild amusement that he'd had a blow-out in the arm pit of his undershirt. She added it to the mental to-do list – she

33

could pick up a new pack of tee shirts for him on her break tomorrow.

Steve disappeared around the corner and she heard the refrigerator door open, the condiment jars clinking. She called after him, "Dinner's on the second shelf."

"Got it," Steve answered, but Jessie heard a can snap open and she knew he'd opted for a beer instead of the macaroni. As far as Jessie could tell after five years of marriage, a beer after work was Steve's one and only vice. He popped back into the living room for just a second to say, "I'm going into the bedroom. I think I can catch the last quarter of the game."

"Okay," Jessie said, watching him disappear down the hall. She knew he'd stop in Ellie's room first, tucking her in if she managed to twist her blankets up since Jessie put her to bed, and by the time she came to bed in an hour or so, the television in their bedroom would be showing the post-game highlights on mute.

For now, she turned her attention back to sewing the last piece of elastic onto Ellie's ballet slipper. It seemed so obvious now, and she felt more than a little embarrassed to be that mom who brings her kid to their first lesson without functional shoes. The heat built in her cheeks a little more as she thought about Melody's fingers brushing over hers as she showed her how to sew the elastics.

Melody probably thought she was an idiot, or an airhead.

Most of the time, Jessie didn't let stuff like that get to her. She'd gotten pregnant at sixteen and left school when her morning sickness came into conflict with the absence policy. For her entire adult life, people had been looking at her like she was stupid because she was a high school drop-out and a teen mother who obviously couldn't figure out how condoms worked. She'd learned pretty quickly that the best thing was just to let those looks and comments roll off her back. But when she thought about how Melody saw her, Jessie suddenly couldn't stand the idea that she might look down on her.

It didn't make any sense at all – their interaction today had lasted all of about ten minutes, and as the receptionist at Ellie's new dance school, Melody should have been one of those background people in Jessie's life who pop up from time to time and rarely elicit more than a friendly smile and maybe a brief conversation about the weather. She shouldn't matter, and Jessie certainly shouldn't be thinking about her so many hours later.

But something in her gut said Melody was different.

Or maybe it was a little lower than her gut. Something clicked on inside her the moment Melody's hand brushed against hers, like an old piece of machinery that was neglected for years and rusted to the point of immobility. Melody was like oil lubricating the gears, setting them in motion again, and it was a sensation that Jessie wasn't totally sure she liked.

In the past five years she'd gotten quite used to being rusty, immobile, and numb. She'd gotten so good at pushing her desires away that she didn't even know she was doing it anymore, and she *always* put Ellie first. Even if Jessie allowed herself to admit how attracted she'd been to Melody, it wouldn't matter because Ellie's happiness was first, last, and only on Jessie's list of priorities.

That's why she married Steve, and why she tried to be a good wife for the last five years. He was a good man who, like her, was doing the best he could to provide for his family – even if he had been a bit of an idiot when they were kids. He'd been the one to tear the condom while he was trying to be a big shot opening the wrapper with his teeth, after all. Meanwhile Jessie had been sixteen, a virgin, and wouldn't have been impressed even if he managed to grow a spectacular pair of tits in the process, but that single act of bravado changed the course of their lives forever.

There didn't seem to be much point in coming out as a lesbian after she took that home pregnancy test and saw those two blue lines, and after the baby came, Jessie didn't have time for girls anyway.

She barely had time to eat, or sleep, and she definitely didn't have time to go back and finish high school. Eventually, though, her life settled into a predictable chaos - a manageable level of disarray. She got used to it, Ellie got used to it, and Steve got used to it.

He got used to her cold shoulder, too. Most of the time Jessie simply told him she was too tired for sex – it was the truth, even if it wasn't the whole truth. The rest of the time, she figured he would just assume she was still a little salty about the whole sixteen-and-pregnant thing. In any case, asexuality had slowly become the norm, and it was a lot easier to get through the day when Jessie couldn't feel anything below the waist.

Melody had been the first girl in a very long time to challenge Jessie's status quo, and as she sat back in her chair, setting down the completed ballet slippers, Jessie closed her eyes and tried to push the thought of Melody away.

CHAPTER SIX

JESSIE

W hen Jessie got home from work, the house was blissfully quiet. Today was her fourth wedding anniversary and Steve had volunteered to pick Ellie up from Jessie's mother's house to save her the trouble. With the extra half hour Steve was saving her, Jessie thought she might take a bath.

She stripped off her repulsive blue vest ('How may I help you?' screen printed on the back in four-inch letters) as she walked down the hall. When she went into the bedroom to hang up the vest, she saw her black knee-length dress laying on the bed and Jessie's first thought was a panicked, "Who died?" But then she noticed a bouquet of wildflowers in a vase on her bedside table along with a note.

I asked your mother to watch Ellie tonight. Put on the dress and be ready by five. We have reservations at your favorite restaurant.

- Steve

Jessie read the note and smiled, her mouth already watering for the gnocchi and sausage at the Italian place Steve was talking about. She couldn't remember the last time they'd eaten at a nice restaurant – it might have been a year ago on their third anniversary.

"You look nice," Steve said when he came home a few minutes before five in a borrowed suit. The sleeves were a half-inch too short, but he cleaned up pretty nice when he wasn't covered in grease from the factory or walking around the house in yellowed tee shirts.

"Back at you," Jessie said as they headed to the car. "You didn't have to do all this."

"I wanted to," he said. "You've been working so hard lately, you deserve a good meal."

The gnocchi was good – incredible, even – and the bottle of wine that Steve splurged on was even better. Jessie didn't realize until she got to the bottom of her second glass that she may have overdone it a little. The restaurant was dark and romantic, candles lighting every table in the intimate dining room, and when she looked at the couples at the other tables, her vision went a little fuzzy.

They looked so in love, staring into each other's eyes, eating off each other's plates, their toes touching and lingering together beneath the tables. The whole damn restaurant was like an advertisement for diamond rings or something.

Jessie watched one particularly amorous couple who

couldn't even bear to eat their entrées without holding hands at the same time, and then she looked across the table at her husband. Steve's eyes were on his plate, completely engrossed in his spaghetti and meatballs. They spent most of the meal talking about Ellie and the process to enroll her in kindergarten, and they hadn't gazed into the other's eyes or touched each other all night.

Not that Jessie wanted to do any of that stuff.

She looked back at the couple, expecting them to go full Lady and the Tramp on a piece of spaghetti at any moment. It was a goddamn miracle that Jessie and Steve had been in the restaurant for a full hour and they hadn't witnessed a proposal yet, and Jessie rolled her eyes as she emptied the dregs of the wine bottle into her glass. She had no use for mushy romance, and she could never figure out why everyone else was so obsessed with it. There was a heartthrob in every movie and a girl waiting for her Prince Charming in every book.

Steve was a good guy but with a little pasta sauce on his chin, he was no Prince Charming and Jessie had no desire to be rescued.

She rolled down the window of Steve's truck on the way home, and by the time they arrived the effects of the wine were wearing off and her head was feeling clearer. The apartment was empty and Jessie and Steve stood in the quiet living room for a moment.

This was about the time that most couples would head for the bedroom together. Jessie wondered if the nauseating ones she'd seen at the restaurant had even made it all the way home before the clothes started coming off.

"I think I'm going to take a bath," Jessie said.

"Okay," Steve answered. "I'm gonna get a beer and find out how the Colts did today."

She headed down the hall and Steve went off toward the kitchen. Jessie stopped in the doorway to the bathroom and called, "Steve?"

"Yeah?"

"Happy anniversary."

"Mm hmm," he said, the crack of the beer can echoing down the hall. "You too, Jess."

CHAPTER SEVEN

MELODY

octor Riley's office was small and dimly lit. There was only one window, high up on the wall, and it always reminded Melody of being in Andy's basement. She sat down in one of the two straight-backed chairs opposite from Dr. Riley's chair. There was an overstuffed armchair in the corner and it looked a lot more comfortable, but Melody didn't like getting too comfortable here. She always sat in the same chair that she'd chosen on her very first visit.

"How are you today, Melody?" Dr. Riley asked. This was more of a small talk question than a serious head-shrinking question. Dr. Riley always opened with it while her back was still turned and she was typing a few notes into the computer on her desk. Melody never knew what these notes were, but she liked to guess sometimes. *Ten minutes late, I could have eaten my lunch slower if I'd known. Tacky shoes today. Don't forget to DVR Grey's Anatomy.*

"I'm fine," Melody said with a shrug. "Got a job last week. How are you?"

"Good," Dr. Riley said, and Melody wasn't sure which of her statements this was a response to. Dr. Riley thrived on vague statements, but at least she never said stuff like, *How does that make you feel?*

Melody's mother had found Dr. Riley for her the same week she came home from New York, doctor's orders, and even though Melody had been unable to persuade her that she didn't need therapy, at least Dr. Riley wasn't totally useless. Melody would never admit it to her parents, but having someone to talk to helped a bit. Melody had seen Dr. Riley every week for six months now, and it was nice to know that no matter what happened during the week, she'd have somebody a little more helpful than Andy to vent it all to.

Her new job, for instance.

"What kind of work are you doing?" Dr. Riley asked as she pulled a legal pad into her lap and then swiveled around in her chair to face Melody. She didn't immediately put the tip of her pen to the page, but Melody knew that she'd be dying to count this as forward progress in her session notes.

"Well, I haven't actually started yet," Melody said. "My first shift is tomorrow. I'm going to be the receptionist at a dance studio."

Dr. Riley's eyebrow ticked up almost imperceptibly, but Melody caught it. Skepticism. Incredulity. She knew it well because that was the same reaction she'd been having herself ever since she accepted Mary Beth's offer.

"How did that come about?" Dr. Riley asked. Given the fact that she'd just spent twenty weeks talking ad nauseam about her traumatic experiences at Pavlova, Melody was expecting a critical reaction like this.

"How do you think?" Melody asked with a wry smile. "Mrs. Bledsoe to the rescue."

"Your mother got you the job?"

"No, she strongly suggested that I get it for myself," Melody explained. "Remember a few weeks ago when I told you that my dad didn't want me sitting around the house anymore? Well, the idea of me finding a job to get back on the horse came up one night over dinner, and I guess it stuck. The next thing I knew I was the front desk girl at Mary Beth's School of Dance."

"Sounds like you may be feeling a little coerced," Dr. Riley suggested.

"You could say that," Melody agreed. "Or trapped, tricked, forced. Any of those words would probably do just as well as any other."

"Is the problem that you don't want to work, or that you don't want to work at a dance studio?" Dr. Riley asked. She jotted a few things down on her notepad, but she was pretty good about doing this sparingly. Melody had a lifetime's worth of people scratching things on notepads while watching her when she was at Pavlova, so Dr. Riley tried to be mindful of how nervous it made her feel.

"I don't mind working," Melody said after considering this question for a moment. "Lord knows my parents paid for enough while I was in New York, and all the lessons before that."

Those words were almost identical to the ones her father had used when he indelicately brought up the subject of work, and close enough to the ones she'd heard a half-million times growing up when they were paying for private lessons and physical therapists and an endless supply of pointe shoes and costumes. In fact, they never let Melody forget how much it all cost.

"So why the dance school?" Dr. Riley asked, putting one finger to the corner of her mouth and propping her chin in her hand the way she did when she thought they were really drilling down to the core of Melody's issues.

She shrugged. "Because they were hiring?"

"There are lots of places around Lisbon that are hiring," Dr. Riley pointed out. "There's nothing preventing you from working somewhere else in town. If you feel trapped when you think about working in a dance school, there are plenty of alternatives out there."

"For a college drop-out who ate, slept, and breathed ballet for the last thirteen years of her life?" Melody asked incredulously. "I can't even make a pot of coffee."

"Okay, so perhaps Starbucks isn't your ideal work-place," Dr. Riley said. "What else would you like to do with your life?"

"I wanted to be a ballerina," Melody said. "That's what I was *supposed* to do with my life."

"Plans change," Dr. Riley said. "Sometimes you just have to roll with the punches and see where your new path is taking you. So, no barista work. What about a doctor's office, or retail, or some kind of trade you could learn with a little bit of training?"

"Gross, boring, and I don't think going into even more debt would make my dad very happy," Melody said. She knew she was being difficult, but the more she thought about her first shift at the dance school, the more irritable she felt. Rather than letting Dr. Riley rattle off a half-dozen more low-paying, entry level jobs, Melody blurted, "I just don't know how I'm going to deal with being surrounded by five-year-old ballerinas all the time. I met one when I applied for the job and it was like looking into a time machine and seeing baby Melody before all the bad stuff happened to her."

Dr. Riley scribbled a quick note. Half the time, Melody was convinced that she was just doodling nonsense on the page in the hopes that Melody would fill the silence and give her more to work with. This time she kept quiet and eventually Dr. Riley said, "Maybe working at the dance school will be therapeutic for you."

"I knew you were going to say that," Melody said. "Andy owes me five bucks now."

"You've been back in Lisbon longer than you were away," Dr. Riley said. "We've been talking for six months about the problems that caused you to leave school and so far we haven't made much headway in helping you move past it. Maybe what you need at this point isn't talk – maybe it's a challenge. Sitting around Andy's basement all day is an avoidance tactic – you know that. Maybe working at the studio will help you confront your demons."

"Sounds like a hoot," Melody said sarcastically.

"I'll be here to help you every step of the way," Dr. Riley said, and Melody wished she was the type of person to find that sort of statement comforting.

She sat back in the stiff chair and tried to picture herself working at a doctor's office, signing patients in and resisting the urge to don a surgical mask every time she heard a wet cough. Even if that did sound tolerable, which it didn't, her first shift at Mary Beth's was tomorrow – considering the utter chaos she'd found the first time she went there, it didn't seem fair to chicken out on such short notice.

AFTER HER THERAPY SESSION ENDED, Melody ended up in Andy's basement once again, avoidance tactic notwithstanding. She found him in much the same place as he'd been the last time she visited, only today it was a different video game and a half-eaten sandwich on the coffee table.

"What are you up to?" Andy asked as she plopped down in her recliner.

"Same old," she said. "Just got back from Dr. Riley's office – she said pay up."

"What's that mean?"

"I bet you five dollars she would say working at Mary Beth's was a good thing, or call it a therapy opportunity, and that's exactly what she did," Melody said with a smirk. She held out her hand and said, "Five big ones, buddy."

"I didn't agree to that bet," Andy said.

"We shook on it," Melody answered. "You were just too stoned to remember."

"Huh," Andy said, looking at the ceiling and contemplating this possibility. Then he shrugged and said, "Well, I don't have five big ones. Guess you're out of luck."

"Jerk," Melody said, crossing her arms over her chest melodramatically.

"I know," Andy said, then a sparkle came to his eyes and he hauled himself off the sunken cushions of the couch. "But I've got something better."

"Better than cold, hard cash?"

"Yep," he said, going over to an old dresser beside his mattress. Melody watched Andy dig a small wooden box out of his sock drawer, from which he retrieved a thin, meticulously rolled joint in a test tube. "Better for you, anyway. Five dollars and a dozen more sessions with Dr. Riley won't fix what ails you as fast as a hit to take the edge off."

He was right about that. Melody wouldn't really call herself a stoner, but she took a hit here and there. The experience of being high was kind of fun – everything in her vision seemed to be clearer and more real, and at the same time more comical – but the day after feeling was the real pay-off. When she smoked, calmness descended on her for about a day after, taking away the anxiety and humiliation of returning home with her head hanging low. It made her life feel temporarily more manageable. Dr. Riley was right - there was only so much that talk therapy could do.

Andy tossed the tube into Melody's lap and she didn't object. The thought of being surrounded by miniature ballerinas all day made her pulse race, and as she picked up the joint she felt a little better just having it in her hand.

"Thanks," she said, tucking it into the pocket of her shirt.

"You should get your shrink to prescribe it to you," Andy said. "It's legal now."

"She's a psychologist, not a psychiatrist," Melody said. "She can't prescribe anything."

"Bummer," Andy answered, and he looked genuinely disappointed on her behalf.

"I should get going," Melody said, getting up from the recliner. "It's almost dinner time."

"Later," Andy said.

Melody went straight up to her room when she got home and stashed the joint in an old school bag at the back of her closet. Maybe she'd smoke it, and maybe she'd forget about it – she hadn't decided yet.

MELODY'S first few weeks at Mary Beth's went by at a dizzying pace. With less than a month before the recital, there were costumes to pick up and tickets to distribute and directions to give. Mary Beth moved through the building like a Tasmanian devil, never staying in one place too long before spinning off to another urgent task. As a result, Melody had to train herself on the finer points of working the front desk.

Most of it was obvious – sign dancers in and point them to the right studio when they arrived for classes, answer the phone when it rang, be pleasant when people walked into the lobby. Some of it was a little more nuanced, like taking payments, but after a short battle with the credit card machine Melody figured that out too, making a list of payments on Post-it notes until Mary Beth had the chance to teach her about the ledgers.

All in all, Melody caught on pretty quickly, and it was fortunate that she was so busy in her first few weeks because it left very little time to even remember the fact that she was working in a dance school. If not for the costumes and the sound of tap shoes clacking on hardwood in the background, she could have been the receptionist at any number of businesses.

Melody didn't feel the urge to smoke the thin joint Andy gave her. She suspected life at Mary Beth's would be tolerable after all, as long as she didn't have to set foot in either of the two studios. That would be too much, too soon.

She liked taking charge of the chaotic reception desk and bringing order to it. She liked watching the kids pour in before big classes, all smiles and energy. But Saturday afternoons quickly became her favorite.

On her first Saturday shift, Melody found herself watching the front door as one o'clock rolled around.

Jessie and Ellie had popped into Melody's head a time or two during the week, and she was looking forward to seeing them again. Unfortunately, Jessie was always coming in at the last possible second and Melody soon learned that their interactions were to be brief. Apart from a few quick words ("Thanks for the tip about those elastics – the slippers work much better now.") Melody didn't see her much before she and Ellie rushed into the studio.

Melody still liked seeing her though. Something about Jessie never failed to make her heart race, even if only for a moment, and she found little ways to prolong them. She would shoot Jessie sultry looks in the second or two of eye contact they enjoyed each Saturday, and usually Jessie looked away but sometimes Melody caught a slight blush coming into her cheeks and a smile on her lips.

Those were the moments that Melody liked best at Mary Beth's.

The ones that proved more challenging were the ones that involved ballet, like the impending recital. Mary Beth expected Melody to come along and be her assistant, making sure all the dancers made their way from the dressing rooms to the stage and back, and that everyone had all the pieces of their costumes.

Melody reluctantly agreed because she couldn't refuse her new employer after less than a month of work, but if Dr. Riley had been able to prescribe her some kind of sedative, she would have taken it for that night. Instead, she dug the joint out of the back of her closet and stuck it in her pocket – not because she was planning to smoke it, but because she felt calmer when she knew it was an option. It was like a safety net.

Mary Beth rented out Lisbon High School's auditorium for the recital, and that was a stage that Melody had danced on many times in her four years there. She remembered the creaky wood floor, and the orchestra pit with its steep drop from the front of the stage - that had been terrifying the first time she saw it during the ninth-grade talent show. There were the heavy velvet curtains and the blinding spotlights, and of course the rows of old theater chairs staring back at her. Melody used to thrive on that sight, and now she just hoped that she could stay far enough in the wings that she wouldn't have to look out and see the audience.

Recital night was just as crazy as everything else Mary Beth did. There were kids running around backstage like banshees and Melody had to chase them all down, group them according to the recital program, and get them into their costumes. This turned out to be harder than it sounded – kids that age grew like weeds and quite a few of them seemed to have grown out of their costumes between the time that they were ordered in the winter and the recital at the end of spring.

"I always tell the parents to order a size larger if their kid is due for a growth spurt, but do they listen?" Mary Beth lamented as she blew through the elementary school-aged dressing room with her clipboard. "Do I have all the intermediate tap dancers? Ladies!"

"They're over there," Melody said with a slight grunt

as she yanked a too-tight purple tutu over the hips of a five-year-old and gestured to a group of girls practicing their choreography in one corner of the room. The girl she was helping whined and tugged at the elastic around her waist, saying it was too tight. Melody turned back to her. "You're dancing right after the tap group – you can take the tutu off in ten minutes."

"Come with me, ladies," Mary Beth said, her voice rising into a shrill sing-song tone. "Melody, can you bring the beginner ballerinas to the stage next?"

"Oh, I don't know," Melody said.

She glanced around the room – there were no less than two dozen dancers under the age of twelve, along with a couple of parents engaged in their own costume struggles. Most of the dance moms had dropped their dancers off at the beginning of the night along with all their costume changes and entrusted Melody and Mary Beth with the task of getting the kids ready to go on stage. This was the least of Melody's reasons for not wanting to escort a dozen ballerinas to the stage, but it was the easiest one to latch onto.

"Someone's got to watch the rest of them," she said, but Mary Beth was already corralling the tap group toward the door. Panic started to rise in Melody's throat.

Mary Beth called to one of the parents across the room, immersed in pinning up her daughter's hair. "Joan, can you take over chaperone duties for a few minutes?"

"Sure," the woman said around a mouth full of bobby pins.

"There you go," Mary Beth said to Melody, and she

was already heading out the door as she called over her shoulder, "Just bring the ones in the purple tutus to the left wing in five minutes."

"Okay," Melody said, but mostly to herself because Mary Beth was long gone by then.

She managed to get all twelve pint-sized ballerinas backstage, although getting there had been a bit like trying to heard cats. Melody wasn't sure how anyone managed to control a single five-year-old, let alone a dozen of them full of energy and adrenaline and ready to dance.

"Shhhh," she said, putting her finger to her lips as she led them up to the door that went backstage. "Once I open this door, you can't talk until you get back into the hallway after your routine. Understand?"

They all nodded, and Melody was surprised at the change that came over them the moment they walked across the threshold. Then again, she could remember her first time backstage – it was cool and dark, and everyone in the wings seemed so important and so focused. There were four thick velvet curtains hanging down from the ceiling, dividing the floor into downstage, center, and upstage, and the way it was lit always looked magical from the darkness of the wings.

Her ballerinas filed calmly into the space behind the middle curtains, where one of Mary Beth's instructors was getting them into position. An old pop song from the eighties was floating through the air and five girls were tapping their hearts out onstage, and with every shuffle ball change, Melody felt her heart thudding faster.

She didn't like the way the metal on their shoes reverberated against the wood floor and echoed into her chest. She didn't like the surreal way the stage lighting looked – in New York, with each failed audition it had begun to take on a fun house quality, the curtains waving more than they should and the spotlights beating down on her, and the feeling was coming back fast.

Melody looked at the beginner ballet class and they were all lining up in order of height thanks to the instructor Mary Beth had enlisted to help out backstage. Thank god she hadn't asked Melody to do that job.

"Hey," Melody whispered to the instructor, inching closer and trying not to look into the audience. "Your name's Emily, right?"

"Yeah," the girl whispered back, both of them trying to keep their voices from echoing into the tall ceiling over the stage.

"I need to get back to the dressing room," Melody whispered. "Can you take it from here?"

"Yeah," Emily said. "Go ahead."

"Thanks," Melody whispered, then headed quickly for the stage door.

The hallway felt bright and large the moment she stepped into it, and it felt good to get away from those tap shoes reverberating in her chest. But every time she tried to take a breath, she found it difficult to fill her lungs. She was taking quick, shallow breaths and everything still looked slightly warped, like the stage lighting. The lockers that lined the hall weren't completely straight, bowing in toward her, and the floor looked warped.

Melody could walk on it okay – there wasn't really anything wrong with it – but she stumbled down the hall nonetheless. When she got to the end, instead of turning right to go into the dressing room, she went straight. There were double doors ahead of her, sunlight streaming through a pair of grimy windows, and her feet propelled her forward. Before she knew it she was outside, sucking in air with her hands on her knees.

After a moment or two she became aware of the fact that anyone standing in the hall and looking out those doors would see her doubled over and gasping like a lunatic, and she was not quite so absorbed in her panic attack that she didn't want to avoid that. Melody took a few steps to the side of the building and leaned against the brick, putting her head back and staring up at the clear blue sky. It was a beautiful day, and here she was losing it over a kids' recital.

Melody thought about the joint that she'd carefully tucked into the back pocket of her jeans in case of exactly this situation. *Smoke in case of emergency.*

Dr. Riley would not be pleased at this choice of coping mechanisms, but Dr. Riley wasn't here right now and she didn't have at least two more hours' worth of little ballerinas to deal with. Melody did, and she reached into her pocket.

CHAPTER EIGHT

MELODY

"*Your turn-out is still not up to par, Ms. Bledsoe.*"

Melody thought she'd be hearing her instructor's sharp voice in her head for the rest of her life. She heard it when she went to bed each night, running through every critique he'd given her that day. She heard it like a refrain during auditions when it should have been just her, the stage, and the music. And she heard it in the endless hours she spent alone in the practice studio each night after everyone else had gone back to the dorms.

"*Straighten that leg!*"

"*Point that toe, Bledsoe.*"

"*You're getting sloppy, Melody. If you can't do it right then just go home.*"

Go home *never meant* go *back to the dorms and rest up a bit. Melody knew that* go home *meant pack your bags and make room for a* capable *dancer to take your place. It was her least favorite of the phrases that ran through her head at all times, the one that filled her most with dread* and drove her back to the practice studio despite hunger, fatigue, injury, or illness.

None of that mattered because she could eat when she was dead. She could sleep when she was dead. She could let her body mend itself when she was dead. She only had one shot at Pavlova, and everything else could wait.

Another one of her instructor's favorite quips, uttered for the first time during Melody's very first class and repeated many, many times since then, was, "You aren't in Lisbon anymore, sweetheart. You're at one of the most prestigious performing arts schools in the country, not some small-town studio. You better start dancing like it."

Pavlova had been a culture shock – that was for sure. Melody was used to getting up early and dancing before school, then coming home and eating a light, protein-rich snack before heading back over to the studio for a couple hours of private lessons. She'd maintained that routine for two years before trying out in New York, and when it paid off she mistakenly believed that she'd done everything she needed to succeed there. She was one of only twenty-four students chosen to enroll that year, and the shock of finding herself in the bottom of every class was difficult to take.

The rest of the Pavlova dancers came from performing arts high schools. They danced their way out of the womb and a lot of them had already performed nationally. And then there was Melody, who to them seemed like a country hick, or maybe just a diversity hire on account of her financial hardships.

She kept trying – nobody put in as much studio time

as she did — and she just kept falling behind with her poor turn-out and sickled feet and small-town, small-time abilities. By the end of her second month, Melody started lying whenever her parents called wanting to know how she was doing and what parts she'd gotten.

"I don't know, the list isn't out yet," she always said, and usually she followed it up with, "Class is about to start. I'll call you later," whether it was true or not.

CHAPTER NINE

JESSIE

Jessie found the recital to be organized chaos. For all of Mary Beth's nervous energy and frantic moments, she had a way of pulling everything together in the end. Ellie was having the time of her life, and that was all that mattered to Jessie.

They spent the first half-hour in the audience, watching the older dancers perform their routines. Jessie watched Ellie out of the corner of her eye at first, and then when she saw how completely absorbed her daughter was, she watched her outright. Ellie was wearing her leotard and ballet slippers despite the fact that she couldn't dance with the other beginning ballerinas – she wanted to at least look like her class-mates, even if her outfit was black and theirs was a shimmering purple.

"Do you want to see if we can find your class?" Jessie whispered after a while, when the parade of kids she didn't know on stage began to blend together. She looked at the program someone handed her as they walked in and told Ellie, "It looks like their number is the one after next. You could wish them luck before they go on stage."

"Yeah," Ellie nodded eagerly. "Let's go."

"Okay," Jessie said. "Just remember we have to be quiet and respectful of the other dancers. Go that way to the aisle and don't make too much noise."

She nodded down the row of chairs, where fortunately no one had chosen to sit beside them. The auditorium was large and it looked like mostly parents and family members in the audience – there were pockets of empty seats here and there, and Jessie was relieved not to have to watch her five-year-old climb over anyone's knees or under their feet to get out.

Jessie followed Ellie up the darkened aisle and out the back door of the auditorium, self-conscious of the light that flooded in from the atrium when they opened the door. Then because she didn't actually know where to find the beginner ballet class, she took Ellie's hand and they wandered through the halls for a little while.

"Look, tap dancers!" Ellie screeched, her voice reverberating down the hall.

"Shh," Jessie implored while Ellie bounced up and down and pointed at a group of girls coming up the hall, led by Mary Beth who looked frazzled to the highest degree.

"Are you on your way to the stage?" Ellie asked them. Jessie grinned – ever the extrovert, Ellie was not afraid to ask anyone anything. She sure didn't get that trait from Jessie, and as long as she remembered the lessons Jessie and Steve had taught her about avoiding certain questions (*"Can I see the puppy in your van?"* and *"What kind of candy you got in there?"* among others) she was happy to encourage her fearless daughter.

"Yep," one of the tap dancers replied.

Mary Beth saw the excitement in Ellie's eyes and paused for a split second to ask, "Do you want to come watch?"

"BACKSTAGE?"

Jessie winced as Ellie did her damnedest to blow out everyone's eardrums, and then she squeezed Ellie's hand in warning. "What did I tell you about using your inside voice?"

"Sorry, mommy," Ellie answered. Then she turned right back to Mary Beth. "Can I?"

"Of course, kiddo," Mary Beth answered with a warm smile. "Do you know the rules of the stage?"

"No talking," Ellie said quickly.

"And stay far back from the curtains so the audience doesn't see you," Mary Beth added. "Well, come on then. The show must go on!"

They followed Mary Beth and the tap group, and Ellie was on cloud nine when they got backstage. Her eyes darted from the pulleys overhead, to the stage, to the tap group getting ready in the wings, to the spotlights hanging from the ceiling over the audience, never resting on any one thing for long because there was too much to take in. Jessie watched her with amusement, and when the tap group shuffled on stage to an old pop song, Ellie stood in the wings, mouth open and totally in awe of the girls.

Jessie hung back, leaning against the wall by the door and taking a moment to breathe. She could only imagine the level of mania Ellie would achieve next year when she actually got to wear a tutu and dance on the big stage with the rest of her class. Jessie would probably have to sedate her afterward or she'd never sleep again after all that excitement.

"Mommy," Ellie said after a minute or two, rushing over to Jessie.

"Quiet."

"Mommy," Ellie repeated at a barely audible whisper. She pointed across the stage to the opposite wing, where Jessie could just make out flashes of purple tulle. "My friends."

"Oh no," Jessie said. "They're on the other side. I don't know how to get to that part of the stage."

"I wanted to wish them luck," Ellie insisted, and she was just bordering on pouty when Jessie realized that there was about three feet of walking room behind the curtain that hung at the back of the stage. Ellie saw her examining it and was immediately onboard. "Can we go?"

"Oh boy," Jessie said, her heart fluttering. "I hope no one can see us walking back there."

"They can't," Ellie said with as much certainty as she could muster. "Let's go!"

Jessie agreed on the condition that they would both walk with their backs to the wall, keeping as much room as possible between themselves and the curtain so as not to create a shadow. They went quickly, Jessie taking Ellie's hand to keep her from getting too excited and accidentally smacking the curtain, and when they got to the other side it was a miracle that she didn't shriek in her excitement at seeing the other girls from her class in their big purple tutus.

"Hi, Ellie," one of the dance instructors said as they approached. Ellie really *did* talk to everyone, because Jessie was pretty sure this girl only taught the advanced classes and she'd only seen her around the school once or twice. The girl asked, "Did you come to watch your class dance?"

"Yes, Miss Emily!"

"I hope it's okay that we went behind the curtain," Jessie said.

"It's fine," Emily said with a shrug. "I've done it at least a dozen times tonight."

The girls on stage tapped their way back into the wings where Jessie and Ellie had just come from, and then it was the beginner ballet class's turn. Ellie sat right down on the floor at the back of the stage, hands on her chin and a huge smile on her face, and Jessie wicked away a few beads of sweat forming on her forehead. It was hot behind those heavy curtains, even without the huge spotlights shining on them.

"You look flushed," Emily whispered to her.

"How do you stand it being back here all afternoon?"

"Lots of water," Emily said, nodding at a bottle on the

floor a few feet away. "You should go get some air – this ancient building isn't air conditioned."

Jessie nodded toward Ellie, but Emily said that she would watch her for a few minutes. Ellie sat like a stone on the floor anyway, and Jessie knew she wouldn't move an inch until her class was done with their routine. She had at least three or four minutes, the length of the song, and it would be nice to go outside and feel the breeze on her face.

"Ellie," she whispered, crouching down beside her. "I'm going outside for just a minute. Emily's here if you need anything, okay?"

Ellie hardly acknowledged her, though – she was absorbed in the dance and gave her mother nothing more than a quick *mm-hmm*. So Jessie went out the way Emily showed her and found a hallway that led to the school's rear parking lot. She went through the doors and took in a deep gulp of the cool spring air.

"Jessie?"

She turned around and leaning against the wall was Melody. She didn't look the greatest, either, her face the inverse of Jessie's – clammy and pale – and there was something slightly panicked in her eyes.

"Melody," Jessie said, shooting her a look of concern. "Are you okay?"

"Super-duper," Melody said, giving her a sarcastic thumbs up.

"What are you doing out here?" Jessie asked, coming over to the wall where she was leaning. "Don't you have to help Mary Beth?"

"Yeah," Melody said. "I have to get back in there."

But she didn't budge from the wall.

"Well, this wall isn't going to hold itself up," Jessie said, leaning against the brick a few feet away from Melody. She had no idea what was wrong with her, if she was sick or if there was something else going on, but Jessie also could not stop the thought that this was the closest they had been to each other since that first day when Melody's fingers brushed her palm.

She suddenly had the urge to reach out and take Melody's hand in hers, just to see if there would be sparks again. Maybe the first time had been a fluke, or maybe they'd picked up a static charge from the carpet when they touched.

That wouldn't explain the way her heart was beating faster now, or the tingling in her belly when she caught herself thinking about lacing her fingers through Melody's.

Melody laughed at her dumb joke, giving Jessie an appreciative little smile and then tilting her head back to rest against the wall. "I came out here because I thought I might puke or pass out or something. I've been having panic attacks lately and they're not exactly a trip to Disney World."

"I always thought the lines and the overpriced food would make the whole vacation fall a bit short of magical," Jessie said. "That's why I'm grateful Ellie hasn't asked to go yet. That, and the fact that I probably couldn't afford to take her even if we both live into the double digits."

"I went to Disney World when I was eight," Melody said, her smile widening just a little more this time. "All I remember was my little sister crying because she loved Goofy on TV but hated him in real life."

"Mmm, like so many men," Jessie mused. "Good in theory, not quite so appealing when you find yourself face to face with them."

Melody gave her a funny look and Jessie blushed furiously. That was definitely a comment she should have kept to herself – it wasn't the kind of thing you said to your background people, but then again this wasn't really the type of situation she usually got into with background people. She never even bothered to learn the names of all the gas station attendants and bank tellers and cashiers that came in and out of her life, let alone started to dig into the messy depths of her psyche for their benefit.

"I mean, that big nose would probably freak me out, too," Jessie added quickly, looking down at the pavement.

"For sure," Melody said. "I don't claim to be an expert on schnozes but that thing has got to be pharmaceutically enhanced."

Jessie had to keep her jaw from dropping at this. Did Melody really just make a dick joke? And was it reading a bit too much into her statement to focus on the part about not being an expert? Jessie cleared her throat and stepped away from the wall.

"So, panic attacks," she said.

"Yeah," Melody answered. "You were doing such a good job of distracting me until you went and brought it up again."

"Sorry," Jessie said, pacing back and forth in front of Melody.

She didn't want to lean against the wall beside her because it seemed impossible to be so close to her and not slide a little closer just to find out if there was a spark. She pictured Melody as a human version of one of those science class plasma globes – an exquisite, olive-skinned and chestnut-eyed version. If Jessie got too close, the lightning inside her would arc and reach for the lightning in Melody, and she didn't know what would happen if they touched.

"So..." Jessie said, reaching for anything at all to say. Everything that came into her head was a double entendre, and she wasn't brave enough to voice any of them.

Luckily, Melody came to the rescue.

"Do you want to smoke a joint?" She blurted. Jessie just looked at her, a little lost, and Melody pulled a little glass tube out of her back pocket. "I was thinking about taking a hit or two before you came out here, to take the edge off."

"Oh," Jessie said. "I don't mind. Do whatever you need to feel better."

"You're not going to tell Mary Beth?"

"No, of course not," Jessie said.

She took a step closer to Melody as she watched her pull the stopper out of the glass tube. Slid into it was a very thin, meticulously rolled joint, and when she opened the tube, a faint skunky smell wafted out. Jessie wrinkled her nose.

"Do you smoke?" Melody asked, pulling a lighter out

of her other pocket and holding the joint between her thumb and forefinger. She was watching Jessie watch her.

"Kinda skipped that part of my teenage years," Jessie said. "Pregnancy can be a bummer for your social life."

"I put my teens off for about five years," Melody said as she put the joint to her lips. Jessie watched them purse around the tip of the joint, unable to tear her eyes away. Melody added, careful not to let the joint slip, "There's no room for the munchies when you're trying to be the next Misty Copeland."

"Wow," Jessie said, and a flash of irritation crossed over Melody's big brown eyes at this blatant show of awe.

"I guess I'm doing all that immature teenager stuff now instead," she said as she flicked the lighter.

The paper at the tip of the joint ignited in a brief flame, then died down as the dried material at the center caught fire. Melody took a quick drag, holding the smoke in her lungs for a few seconds before tilting her head back and exhaling a long plume of smoke into the air above their heads.

She saw Jessie watching her intently and held the joint out to her. "Want to help me make up for lost time?"

The idea of doing anything with Melody made something tingly rise in Jessie's stomach – she thought this must be the sensation people got when they talked about butterflies – but at the same time, something in her chest told her to go back inside and focus on her first and only goal, Ellie. The beginner ballet class was probably finished dancing by now, and without intervention Ellie would be following them back to the dressing rooms and making a pest of herself.

Jessie really should think of her parental duties.

For just a second though, she looked at Melody leaning against the brick wall of the high school that Jessie dropped out of five years earlier, and she imagined what it would be like to say yes. There was something happening here and Jessie didn't want to leave now.

With her heart pounding, she reached out and took the joint. Her fingers brushed against Melody's, and the only thing she could think of as she looked at it pinched between her thumb and forefinger was that this was so very unlike her.

"How long will it last?"

"About an hour if you're lucky," Melody said. "It's not very good weed."

"Will Ellie notice?"

"Not unless you're planning to smoke the whole thing," Melody said with a smile.

She was amused at Jessie's complete lack of experience, and Jessie couldn't help thinking it was a bit charming the way Melody's dimples became more pronounced when she smirked at her.

Melody turned to face Jessie, her shoulder still leaning against the brick wall, and it seemed like the space between them was shrinking every minute. Their eyes met, and Jessie allowed herself to linger openly over Melody's face for the first time. Her tongue flicked briefly over her lips, her teeth biting into her fleshy lower lip as a smile played over her face, and then she said, "Maybe take a small hit just to see what it's all about."

Jessie put the joint to her lips and followed along with Melody's instructions.

"Suck the smoke into your mouth, and then inhale it into your lungs. You might cough," she said, watching Jessie intently the whole time. The smoke was acrid but she managed not to choke on it like a complete idiot. Melody grinned and said, "But probably not because this is some pretty weak stuff. Okay, now exhale."

Jessie tilted her head up the same way Melody had, blowing her first hit of weed skyward, then she handed the joint back to Melody, who was still looking at her expectantly.

They were silent for a moment, and then she said, "I don't feel anything."

Melody took a second hit, then brushed the joint against the brick until the burning tip fell to the pavement. "Give it a minute."

Jessie watched her pinch the tip of the joint, checking to make sure it had gone out, and then pull the glass tube back out of her pocket to carefully put it away. Melody's fingers were so slender and yet they moved so adeptly at her task. Jessie found herself blushing as she wondered what else those fingers could do, and then Melody was laughing.

"What?"

"Don't look now, but you're a little stoned."

"I am?"

"You were watching my hands as if I was performing

brain surgery," Melody said. "Yeah, I'm pretty confident. How does it feel?"

Jessie tore her eyes away from Melody's fingers as she stuffed the joint back into her pocket. She looked around, at the motionless parking lot and the expanse of asphalt, and then at the way the sun glittered through the leaves of a nearby oak tree, and the feeling of the breeze on her skin. It was all exactly the same as it had been when she came out here, but slightly different in a way she couldn't really put into words.

She looked at Melody and something in her chest swelled with joy. Aside from the precious few moments she got to spend with Ellie in the evenings, seeing this girl was the highlight of her week. Now *that* was an effect of being high, perhaps, because Jessie never would have admitted that, even to herself, if she was in her right mind.

"You're beautiful," she said before her filter had a chance to catch up to her mouth.

And then, before her brain had a chance to catch up to her body, she watched Melody lean over to kiss her. She watched Melody's dimples deepen, then those beautiful chestnut eyes came closer and closer, and Jessie could smell strawberries in her hair and peppermint balm on her lips. They were just inches from Jessie's and she wanted nothing more than for them to meet, but at the last second, she came to herself again and stepped away.

"I'm sorry," Jessie said, but before she had a chance to say what she was sorry for, the door banged open behind them.

"Break's over," Mary Beth said loudly to Melody. "We need you in there."

No sooner had she made her announcement than Mary Beth whirled around and went back inside, the door swinging shut behind her.

"I- I gotta go," Melody said with an apologetic smile. "Thanks for talking me down from my panic attack – I feel a lot better now."

It occurred to Jessie to say something slick, like *so do I*, but Melody was already gone by the time she came up with the words, and it was probably better that she didn't say anything. She stood outside for a few more seconds, taking deep gulps of the cool breeze and feeling the tingle of Melody's peppermint balm on her lips. She looked into the oak tree and the leaves were just leaves again. Maybe there was nothing to that single hit of weed after all – maybe Melody was the reason she felt different.

WHEN JESSIE FOUND ELLIE, she was backstage whispering excitedly to Mary Beth while the poor woman tried to organize a half-dozen dancers in the wings.

"I'm going to be in the number next year," she was chattering at Mary Beth as Jessie approached, hoping that the skunky pot smoke had not permeated her clothes.

"Come on, bug, you're talking her ear off," Jessie said, taking Ellie's hand. She turned to Mary Beth and tried not to look too guilty as she said, "Thanks for letting her watch from the wings. I hope she wasn't too much trouble."

"On the contrary, kiddo," Mary Beth said as she waved her next set of dancers onto the stage. She turned to Jessie and said, "I saw some natural talent in your daughter. She seems to have an eye for the choreography."

Jessie looked at Ellie, who was smiling from ear to ear at this complement despite the fact that Jessie was about ninety percent sure she hadn't yet learned the meaning of the word 'choreography'. She asked Mary Beth, "Is that so?"

"When her class went onstage, Ellie stood in the wings and I watched her do the routine along with them," Mary Beth said. "Of course she doesn't have the technique down yet, but that just takes practice. Ellie, it's too bad you didn't enroll soon enough to order a costume or you could have been out there dancing this year."

"Well, she has spent just about every waking moment in her ballet slippers since we started coming to class, so I'm not surprised," Jessie said with a proud smile.

Mary Beth winked at Ellie, then told Jessie, "She'll have to start in the beginner ballet class in the fall, but I don't know if that'll be much of a challenge for her. I bet she'd really benefit from one-on-one lessons with a private instructor."

Jessie saw Ellie's eyes lighting up at this idea – she'd only been to four lessons, but already she was making friends in that class. It was Jessie's fault for not having the heart to tell Ellie that she'd have to wait til fall to start classes, and it would mean a lot to Ellie, bragging rights notwithstanding, to get one-on-one attention like that.

"Private lessons... I don't know if that's in the budget-" Jessie began, not eager to have this conversation from the wings of the stage. She'd have to break the news to Ellie later in the evening, once they got home.

"I have to go get the next group," Mary Beth cut in.

"Of course," Jessie said, feeling guilty for taking up so much of her time. Had she been rambling? Was that a lingering effect of the pot?

"But don't discount it simply because money is an issue," she said, shooting another encouraging look to Ellie. "Call me once classes start up again and maybe we can work something out."

CHAPTER TEN

MELODY

Melody drove her father's car home after the recital ended. It was dark by the time she finally finished vacuuming glitter and sequins off the dressing room carpet, and even though she'd looked for her, Melody didn't run into Jessie again.

She figured Jessie and Ellie went home after the beginner ballet class performed their number, and they were lucky to have an excuse to leave. The couple of hits she'd taken from Andy's joint had helped calm her nerves, but for some strange reason, she found Jessie's presence even more calming. As a result, she could feel her absence all the more keenly, and she wondered what exactly was happening between the two of them. She had never felt her heart pulling so strongly toward someone before.

Melody's parents were waiting for her when she got home. She would have preferred to go straight upstairs to her room, or maybe into the bathroom for a soak in the tub where she'd do her damnedest not to let her mind wander to the way it felt to be but inches away from Jessie's plump lips. Instead, her mother called her to dinner.

She came obediently into the dining room, where she found her father already sitting at the head of the table and her little sister, Starla, sitting with her hands folded on the table in front of her.

"The meatloaf went cold," Starla said with a snotty tone as Melody sat down across from her and their mother started passing the dishes around.

"I didn't ask you to wait for me," Melody said. "I was working."

"Be nice, you two," her father barked as he took a plate of mashed potatoes. He plopped a generous spoonful onto his plate and asked, "How's that going, by the way?"

Oh boy, Melody thought, a heaviness settling on her chest like it always did when she and her parents had a 'serious talk'. *Here we go.*

"It's actually going okay," she said grudgingly while Starla passed her the meatloaf, which had indeed become lukewarm.

Melody didn't want to tell her parents that life at Mary Beth's turned out *not* to be one long torture scene as she'd predicted to them – and to Dr. Riley – that it would be. Then she would have to admit that it hadn't been a mistake to apply there, and that she *was* ready to take at least a few tentative steps toward figuring out her life again. Just the thought of admitting it made her feel like hyperventilating.

But since she couldn't outright lie to them, she settled on selective truth-telling. "I had a panic attack at the recital tonight and had to go outside for a breather."

She didn't mention the pot, or Jessie's strange calming effect on her. She definitely didn't mention the fact that they'd almost kissed, or the fact that it was all she could think about since then.

"Oh, honey," her mother said, reaching across the table to pat Melody's hand. "Well, you got through it. That's the important thing."

"She got through something that she used to do every day of her life for hours and hours," Starla said, rolling her eyes in the severe way that only a fourteen-year-old girl is capable of. "Let's give her a medal already."

"Star," their mother snapped, and Starla shut her mouth, looking down at her dinner plate and picking at the somewhat congealing meatloaf.

"Well, I'm glad to hear that it's going well," their father said, bringing the conversation back around to what was most important to him – responsibility. "Do you think there's any chance of getting promoted to a full-time position, Mel? You know, with benefits, a raise?"

"Mom," Melody said plaintively, turning to her mother for backup. She'd always come down on the side of helpful, where her father was more or less always on the nagging end of things. "I'm going to help you guys pay back those loans, but I'm doing everything I can right now."

"Give her a little more time, Frank," her mother scolded, but her father was on a tear and nothing was going to stop him now that he got going.

Melody glanced over at Starla, who was eating her cold meatloaf with a small smirk on her face. She'd lived her entire life in the shadow of her big shot ballerina sister, and now that Melody had come home in disgrace, she never missed an opportunity to rub salt in the wounds.

"She's almost nineteen years old," her father pointed out. "She should be finishing her first year of college right now, not starting over from scratch and working part-time at a minimum wage job."

"Plans change," Melody muttered, a line that Dr. Riley was fond of in their sessions but which did little to assuage her father's objections.

"You're right, honey, they do," he said, taking in a deep breath, and she knew exactly what was coming next.

Second behind his desire for her to find full-time work that could feasibly turn into a career was his desire for her to go back to Pavlova so that all the time and money they invested in her when she was a kid wouldn't go to waste. She didn't like to think that her father saw her as a poor investment, but when he talked like this, it was hard not to see it. She braced for it.

"You could go back," he said. "You could meet with your instructors and work out a plan to get up to speed for the fall, make up the classes you missed last semester and catch up to your class."

"I wasn't up to speed when I was *there*," Melody pointed out through gritted teeth. "That was the whole problem."

"The problem was that you threw in the towel," Frank said, his voice edging slightly closer to frustration, and Melody didn't want to have this conversation yet again.

She couldn't have it right now, not when she really was making progress with Dr. Riley and things were going okay at Mary Beth's. She couldn't have it when things were just beginning to make sense again and Jessie was in the back of her mind. She stood up from the table.

"I did throw in the towel, and I'm retired from dance," Melody said for about the hundredth time. "If somebody in this family has to be a ballerina, it's going to have to be Starla. Or you."

Melody stomped out of the dining room – turning into a petulant teenager yet again. She felt helpless and powerless so often now that she was back in Lisbon, living under her parents' roof with the acute awareness that she had no other choice and no refuge except Andy's basement. It regressed her and she didn't even care that she was ruining dinner as she stormed out of the house.

How many times did she need to explain to her father that no one gets a second chance at Pavlova? Even if she wanted to return to New York and beg everyone she knew at that school to let her back in, it would never happen. She'd been absurdly lucky to be one of the twenty-four admitted in the first place, and then she'd fallen to pieces and ruined it all.

Melody's days as a dancer were done.

She headed outside and didn't even think about where she was going. On muscle memory, her legs carried her up the sidewalk and a few houses over to Andy's place. It was like the hundreds of arabesques she'd done in her life. She never had to check in the mirror to make sure her leg was parallel to the ground or her toes were pointing out like they should – she could do a perfect arabesque in her sleep – or so she'd thought until her confidence was shattered in New York.

Now, her big trick was that she could walk blind-folded to Andy's basement - she'd come to know the route so well in the last six months.

"Hey," she said as she came down the steps and found Andy right where she'd left him, sitting on the couch with an assortment of food littered around him and a game controller in his hands. "You should get up and move around sometimes or you'll get bedsores."

"Would you be my nurse if I did?" he asked, and Melody made a retching sound.

"Barf," she said as she sat down in her customary recliner. He nodded toward the bong, his version of hospitality, but she waved it away. "I'm good. You know, my parents think you're a bad influence."

"Because of the weed?"

"Because you have no 'aspirations' for your life."

"Sheesh," Andy said. "I'm feeling attacked. Tell me, how else am I a piece of shit?"

"I'm sorry," Melody relented. "My dad got on my

case again about finding a full-time job, or a purpose or something."

"And I have to bear the brunt of your anger?" Andy asked. "I'll have you know that I do have aspirations."

"Yeah? What are they?" Melody asked, looking curiously at him.

"Get high, get laid, get to level fifty," he said, ticking them off on his fingers.

"You're a walking stereotype," Melody said with a groan.

"Maybe, but I'm two thirds of the way to living the dream."

"Let me guess which goal is lagging," Melody said with a roll of her eyes.

"And you're a regular lady Casanova," Andy said. "Those in glass houses..."

"I'll have you know I *almost* got to first base today," she said a little cockily as she thought about Jessie.

Andy looked surprised, but he laughed. "Well, look at you."

Melody sat back in the recliner, glancing over at the television, which Andy switched over to old cartoon reruns. If he wasn't playing video games then he was watching cartoons, the perpetual man child. Maybe her parents were right about one thing.

CHAPTER ELEVEN

JESSIE

J essie spent the summer working long hours at both the grocery store and the diner. She figured that Ellie's three months off from dance would be as good a time as any to bank some extra money and make sure they'd have enough to cover a full year of dance lessons. She'd balked when Mary Beth suggested that Ellie should take private lessons, but she'd quietly decided to start saving toward that goal in case Ellie really got into ballet and Mary Beth still thought she'd be advanced enough to catch up with the intermediate class this year.

Besides, the busier she kept herself, the less time there was to think about what had happened between her and Melody in the parking lot at the recital. She walked outside and the moment she saw Melody, Jessie turned into a dumb teenage girl. What was that all about? There had definitely been sparks, and she hadn't stopped feeling guilty about that fact ever since.

Jessie felt sick whenever she thought about Melody and then thought of Steve. The way their sex life was – nonexistent – she'd be shocked to find out that Steve never looked at women. But Jessie couldn't fathom life without him, and how much more complicated things would be if she had to juggle her jobs, Ellie's education, dance lessons, and visitation with Steve on top of all that. Jessie wasn't even sure if she could support the two of them on a pair of minimum wage jobs.

Even more than all of these hypothetical scenarios running through her head, though, Jessie was afraid because Melody had turned something on inside of her that she'd been trying very hard to keep turned off.

The moment her lips drew close, Jessie's stomach stirred, her thighs got warm and tingly, and she felt something that she long ago wrote off as dead. It was the price she paid to maintain a civil, functional marriage with Steve and provide a good life for Ellie, and it had seemed like a pretty minor sacrifice to her until she met Melody.

Jessie always abided by that old adage, you can't miss what you never had, and in the rare moments when she and Steve kissed and she felt nothing, she had tried to convince herself that kissing just wasn't her thing. There were no fireworks or butterflies or any of the other cliché, stupid things that the people in movies and romance novels described, and eventually she and Steve stopped bothering with each other so none of it mattered anyway. There was no point in coming out about her sexuality, even to herself, when she was determined to keep her family together for the sake of her daughter. She could live without sex, and even without love, as long as she had Ellie to pour her heart into.

The moment Melody entered Jessie's personal space, though, all of that changed. They hadn't even kissed – their lips wisped by each other in an instant without touching – but already she felt more than she'd ever felt for Steve. She knew what people meant by the butterflies and the fireworks now, and her world erupted into vibrant color. It was like she'd been living in black and white and didn't know any better until Melody introduced her to sensual blue and carnal red and graceful yellow. And rich chestnut brown, oh that chestnut brown.

At the end of the day, though, it didn't matter.

Jessie might be awoken to the beautiful things in the world that she was missing, but nothing about her situation changed because of this revelation. It was like a sick joke that the universe played on her – there were a lot of those in her life. Pregnant at sixteen. Pregnant the first time she had sex. Figured out she was gay in the same moment she realized her life was tied inexorably to Steve. And now, fell in love with a girl she could never have.

The only thing Jessie could do to combat this was keep herself busy. This wasn't hard given her schedule, but even working eighty hours a week wouldn't have kept her mind from drifting back to Melody. She found herself thinking about her in all of the quiet moments of her day.

There were the lulls between customers while she

was working the cash register at the grocery store. She liked her shifts at the diner better because they kept her mind more occupied. She had to take orders and attend to her customers and deliver food and bus her tables. There wasn't a lot of time to sit around and think about the lunacy of pining for a girl she barely knew.

Cashiering, on the other hand, wasn't exactly mentally taxing work, and it left her mind free to roam. Hell, that task required so little brain power that most of the time she could slip into a fully-formed fantasy world while her hands kept mechanically swiping canned goods across the scanner.

It was a bad idea to indulge these thoughts – Jessie knew the only thing she could accomplish with them was to dig herself even deeper into her desire for Melody. But after a few weeks of trying to fight it, her mind started subtly protesting. Jessie could never threaten Ellie's peace by uprooting her world and going after Melody, but she also couldn't stop herself from imagining how life might have turned out differently. What if she'd kissed Melody when they were alone together at the recital? What if she'd never agreed to go on a date with Steve at all? What was the harm in imagining it?

So one Tuesday morning when the store was particularly slow and she hadn't seen a customer in fifteen minutes or more, Jessie let her guard down. She wondered if Melody ever shopped here – Lisbon wasn't a big city, after all – and what she'd do if suddenly Melody stepped into her checkout line.

"Hi," she'd say, giving Jessie a little smirk in the seductive way she had.

"Hey," Jessie would respond, and in her fantasies every bit of the anxiety she felt when Melody was around melted away. She'd be confident and cool. "Come here often?"

"No," Melody would say as she came closer, her eyes never moving from Jessie's. "I just came to pick up one thing."

"What's that?" Jessie would ask, and Melody wouldn't stop when she came to the credit card machine like her customers always did.

She'd keep walking, her eyes locked on Jessie's and her hips swaying in a sultry way as she came around the end of the register and stepped into Jessie's space. Their bodies would nearly touch – just a sliver of air between them – and Jessie would feel Melody's breath, hot and peppermint-laced like it had been at the recital, as she whispered, "*You*."

The rest of Jessie's fantasy tended toward the explicit. On different days, depending on how voracious she was feeling, she'd pick Melody up and set her on top of the scanner, her register beeping with confusion as Jessie wrapped her arms around her and kissed those luscious lips passionately. Or they'd lay down on the belt, knocking all the little impulse buys – gum and mints and candy bars – to the floor as their bodies pressed together. Or Melody would simply drop to her knees and her fingers would reach for the button of Jessie's khakis–

"Excuse me!"

This was usually how her fantasies ended, with a grumpy old man or a housewife bogged down with kids bringing her back to reality and the realization that a line had formed in front of her register. Jessie would blush furiously and hope to hell her face didn't tell everyone exactly what she'd been thinking about, then she'd promise herself that she wouldn't think about Melody again.

After a few weeks of this new reality, Jessie was starting to realize how empty that promise was.

When her grocery store shift came to a merciful end a little before dinner time one day, Jessie thought she'd make a quick run home to fix herself a peanut butter sandwich and see Ellie for twenty minutes or so before her shift at the diner started. She'd been pulling doubles for a couple of months, and she usually came home in the hour between her two jobs just to check in on everyone.

That day, though, the idea of looking Steve in the eyes so soon after she'd laid Melody down on the conveyor belt in her mind seemed impossible. The fantasy was too fresh and Jessie's cheeks were even a little flushed. Jessie wanted to see Ellie – she'd be in bed by the time Jessie came home tonight – but the shame of what she'd been doing with Melody in her mind trumped this desire.

She climbed into her rusted-out Sebring at the back of the parking lot and the door swung noisily shut. Jessie spent two years babysitting and saving her birthday money to buy that car when she turned sixteen, and it had been an old rust bucket even back then. Now that she was twenty-two, it might qualify as an antique if it wasn't composed almost entirely of duct tape and prayers. It still got her where she needed to go, though, and now she chugged her way down the street to McDonald's.

It was frivolous to eat out when there was a perfectly good peanut butter sandwich waiting for her at home, especially when the whole reason she was killing herself with the double shifts was to save money for Ellie's private lessons. But if she wasn't going home she'd have to find something, and Jessie decided it was okay as long as she ordered off the dollar menu.

It wasn't that she and Steve were destitute – they had two working vehicles, a roof over their heads, and all the sports channels Steve wanted. But every dime of Jessie's two jobs and Steve's factory position went into maintaining that kind of lifestyle.

She pulled up to the drive-through and a muffled voice said, "Welcome to McDonald's, how can I help you?"

There was absolutely nothing welcoming about that monotonous voice. Maybe it was the ancient, tinny speaker playing tricks, but Jessie found that doubtful.

"Hi, can I get a McChicken and small fries, please?" Jessie called, and she always had to shout through the damn things just to be heard. She figured having orders screamed at them all day probably didn't give the person on the other end of the speaker much reason to be jovial.

"Two dollars, next window."

Jessie did as she was instructed, thinking that life

could be worse. She could be the monotonous voice at the other end of the McDonald's speaker, saying the phrase 'next window' about two hundred times a day.

Back in her carefree early teens, before Ellie – before the possibility of getting pregnant had even occurred to her – Jessie was just a regular kid with her life ahead of her. Jessie's parents weren't wealthy, but everyone thought she would go to college, maybe on a scholarship. People never asked her *if* she wanted to go, but rather *where* or *for what*.

But then she got knocked up, and everything changed.

Jessie knew a seventeen-year-old with a newborn and half of a high school education wasn't the most coveted applicant in the job market, but she had no way of guessing just how hard it would be to find decent work without a diploma. Jessie tried to go back to school when Ellie was a baby, attending night school and studying in the brief moments when Ellie was asleep or otherwise occupied, but then came potty training and daycare costs and a million other excuses to give up. She did, putting Ellie first. Even if she'd succeeded and earned her GED, she knew it would only qualify her to work a job with slightly more responsibility at the grocery store, or some repetitive, entry-level job in an office where she couldn't afford the business casual wardrobe or take time off when Ellie got sick.

Decent jobs with full-time hours and benefits seemed forever out of her reach, but as she pulled up to the next window and saw the sullen face of the McDonald's cashier, Jessie had to be thankful knowing that things could always be worse. She took her McChicken and fries and sat in the parking lot to eat and wait for her next shift to start, and she felt more determined than ever to keep Melody as a fantasy and nothing more. She had too much to lose.

CHAPTER TWELVE

JESSIE

Their first apartment was nothing more than a spare room over a garage. Jessie found it in the classified ads while she was waiting for her final ultrasound before the baby came. She had to hold the paper at arm's length just to turn the pages around her belly, and she'd been looking for apartments for weeks with no luck.

When she found this one, though, she thought it might work. Just over a hundred and fifty square feet, there was barely enough room to move around, but it was furnished, it had its own bathroom and a kitchenette, and at a hundred and fifty bucks a month, she and Steve could afford it.

The day they moved in was the day Jessie and Ellie were released from the hospital, and she had never been more terrified in her life. She cradled the squirming, softly crying bundle in her arms while Steve drove his old truck across town at five miles under the speed limit, looking over frequently to check on the two of them.

"This is it?" He asked as Jessie directed him to park on the street in front of the house.

He was still going to high school during the days and he'd taken a second shift job in the factory where his dad worked, so he never got to see the apartment before Jessie signed the lease, and she caught the disappointment in his voice as he sized it up from the street.

"It was all we can afford," she said, not taking her eyes off Ellie's tiny features. "We'll make it a home."

For the first time since she discovered that she was pregnant, Jessie found that she wanted to build a family with Ellie's father. Sure, he'd never made her heart sing or made her see fireworks when they touched. In fact, they hadn't touched much at all since the night Jessie got pregnant. But there was more to a family than sex, and looking into Ellie's wide, curious eyes, Jessie wanted to do everything she could to make a home for her daughter.

Steve came around the truck and opened Jessie's door, taking the baby in his arms. She grimaced as she hauled herself out of the truck– Ellie was only two days old and everything about Jessie's seventeen-year-old body felt like it was about ninety-five today. She was grateful when Steve carried Ellie, and even more so when he held out his arm for Jessie to lean on as they hobbled together up to the house. There was an indoor stairwell, a necessity with an infant to think about – no icy metal stairs to fall down in the winter – and it took Jessie a good two or three minutes just to make it to the top.

When they got there, she unlocked the door and let it

swing open, holding her breath in anticipation as Steve's eyes swept over the small space.

"Home sweet home," she said meekly, waiting for his reaction.

"Yeah," he said, stepping into the space that would become their bedroom, living room, dining room, and kitchen for the next eighteen months before Jessie was able to start working and they finally saved enough money to rent a decent apartment. He looked down at his daughter in his arms and cooed, "What do you think of your new home, bug?"

Jessie stood in the doorway for a moment, resting her shoulder against the door frame and catching her breath from the climb. She smiled as she watched her new husband showing their infant daughter around the little room. This wasn't the life she wanted – not by far – but it could have been a lot worse.

CHAPTER THIRTEEN

MELODY

Mary Beth's was closed for the summer and Melody couldn't imagine her boss being any more calm on vacation than she was at work – she pictured Mary Beth on an island somewhere in the Caribbean, going nuts and driving the hotel staff crazy with demands and questions.

Whether Mary Beth was relaxing or bothering the hell out of a cabana boy somewhere tropical, Melody found herself with a lot of time on her hands again. She'd gotten used to her schedule at the reception desk, and even though she was only working fifteen hours a week, it had given her a sense of purpose. She never would have admitted this to anyone except Dr. Riley, but it felt nice to have a reason to get dressed in something other than pajamas.

Now, though, she wiled away the days much the same way she had before her parents forced her into employment – in Andy's basement. They smoked and snacked and watched television and bullshitted until it was time to go home and have dinner each evening, and Melody spent a fair amount of time thinking about Jessie.

She always breezed into the lobby so last-minute, ushering Ellie into the studio and barely stopping at the reception desk to scribble her daughter's name on the sign-in sheet, so Melody had no idea when she'd get her next opportunity to relive their little moment outside of the school. She just knew that she had to find a way. She found herself daydreaming on more than one occasion about the two of them alone at the desk, her hand lingering over Jessie's as she passed her a pen to sign in, and then grabbing her by the wrist and pulling her over the counter to finally have that kiss.

By the time the school opened again in the middle of July, Melody had lived a thousand fantasy lives with Jessie, and even Andy was beginning to find her romanticism of their shared joint during the recital to be a bit obsessive.

"Try not to expect too much," he warned her one night before classes started up again. "Maybe it didn't mean anything to her."

"It did," Melody objected. "I could tell."

She resisted the urge to make another wise-crack about Andy's inexperience with women, especially considering the fact that Melody wasn't much better off. She'd kissed a few girls in high school, and once during a pep rally, a girl from her science class pulled her under the bleachers and Melody found out what second base felt like, but since then her experience with women dwindled down to almost nothing. There just wasn't time for anything except dance and sleep and more dance when she was in New York.

On Saturday morning, Melody reported to work feeling a lot more nervous than she'd ever felt standing behind the reception desk. It wasn't the same kind of anxiety that bubbled up when her mother suggested she work at a dance school, or the panic that built in her chest when she stood in the wings of the Lisbon High School auditorium last month.

This was more like butterflies in her stomach, and clammy palms, and the kind of lovesickness you get when you know you're about to see your crush after a long time apart.

She tried to keep herself occupied, but aside from welcoming everyone back to Mary Beth's, reminding them about the sign-in sheet, and taking payments from new dancers, the majority of Melody's morning was spent pushing away memories of all the fantasy kisses she'd shared with Jessie in her head. After a summer apart, a summer spent dreaming about the moment when they would reunite, it was hard to divorce reality from fantasy and remember that there had only been the build-up to a kiss, and that it was pretty quick at that.

It was just one moment, and it might not have meant anything, Melody reminded herself as she heard the door open and Ellie came dashing in.

"Miss Melody!" She shrieked excitedly, bounding across the lobby.

Even as Ellie came around the desk and Melody

stooped down to give Ellie a quick hug, she could not subscribe to her own mantra. It was just a few minutes alone, but it meant something. Every time she shared a room with Jessie, her whole body felt electrified and her heart swelled and she craved Jessie's lips. It wasn't nothing.

"Welcome back!" Melody exclaimed to Ellie, who seemed to have grown in the month since the recital. Melody was a little surprised to find that she was genuinely excited to see the girl, as well as her mother. "How was your break?"

"It was great," Ellie said. "I practiced every day!"

"She sure did," Jessie's voice came over the counter, and Melody turned to face her.

A little part of her was afraid that when she looked at Jessie, all of the magic would fall away and the moment wouldn't live up to the fantasy version that Melody had constructed over the past few weeks. She was afraid that Jessie wouldn't be as mesmerizing as she remembered, or else Melody would find that she preferred the fantasy version she'd built instead of the real thing.

But there was no universe in which Jessie Cartwright in the flesh wasn't the best possible reality. If anything, she looked better than she had a few months ago, the summer sun bringing color to her cheeks and making her red hair even more radiant than before, with little streaks of copper running through it. Melody bit her lip – she couldn't help it – and a flash of desire ran unmistakably through Jessie's eyes, too.

But then those mossy pools darkened and went flat.

Melody watched as all the expression drained out of Jessie's face, as if on purpose, and she pointed mechanically to the sign-in clipboard. "Same process as last year?"

"Umm, yeah," Melody said.

She grabbed a pen from the desk and held it out to Jessie, ready to play out the fantasy that she'd dreamed so frequently over the summer. Maybe they couldn't kiss right now – not with Ellie standing nearby – but Melody would enjoy the feeling of their fingers brushing over each other almost as much.

Jessie barely acknowledged Melody's outstretched hand, though. She grabbed another pen that someone had left on the ledge of the reception desk instead and printed Ellie's name on the sheet. Melody cursed herself for not having kept the desk clear, and then Jessie was holding her hand out for Ellie.

"Come on, I'm going to help you put your slippers on and then I have to run an errand for daddy while you're in class, remember?" She asked as Ellie took her hand and they headed toward the studio with not so much as a glance back toward the desk.

Melody was left with a pen in her hand and a confused look on her face. She had no idea what had gone wrong, and even if Andy had been right that their moment during the recital didn't mean anything to Jessie, she'd never expected this outright coldness. Jessie barely even looked at her.

THE BEGINNER BALLET lesson was almost finished by the time Jessie returned. Melody had spent the hour listening to the pitter-patter of a dozen slipper-clad feet dancing across the floor to *Fur Elise,* a classical number she'd danced a time or two herself.

There was nothing to do at the reception desk since the next class didn't start for another forty-five minutes, and she didn't want to dwell too much on Jessie's quick departure. Instead, she tried to pick out Mary Beth's choreography based on the sounds of the girls' feet.

This proved particularly challenging given the fact that the class was full of five- and six-year-olds who weren't very good at executing the steps yet, but Melody needed a challenge right now to keep her mind off everything it wanted to fixate on. Jessie always did blow in and out of the dance school like a tornado, and maybe it didn't mean anything, but by the way Jessie wouldn't even look her in the eyes, she got the impression that she was being willfully ignored. Melody closed her eyes and tried to decide if the brushing motion she heard was a jeté or a glissade.

She'd just about settled on jeté when a familiar, velvety voice said, "Hi."

Melody jerked her eyes open, startled, and saw Jessie standing on the other side of the reception desk. She was alone in the lobby when she closed her eyes and didn't hear Jessie enter.

"Sorry, did I scare you?" She asked, a delicate blush rising into her cheeks momentarily.

"Yeah," Melody said, "But that's okay."

She smiled, then glanced toward the closed studio door. There were about five minutes left in the class and this might be the moment she'd been waiting for – her opportunity to finish the kiss that had gotten away from her in the spring.

Melody stood up, but Jessie took a tentative step away from the desk.

"I'm back earlier than I expected," she said. "It would be rude to interrupt the class now to go sit with the other moms."

"Yeah, you're probably right," Melody said, and she took a step toward the end of the reception desk. She wanted nothing more than to walk around the desk and pull Jessie into her arms. "You should stay here with me."

Jessie's eyes grew a little larger as she watched Melody coming around the desk, and she sank down into one of the chairs lining the wall beside the reception desk. "I'm just going to sit here and wait if that's okay."

Then she looked away, toward the window at the front of the lobby. It seemed like a pretty pointed gesture, and Melody sank disappointedly back into her chair. Did she do something wrong?

They sat in silence for a few minutes, the cool-down music that Mary Beth always used filtering into the little lobby and doing nothing to cut the tension between them. It was obvious that Jessie was ignoring Melody on purpose, keeping her head turned as far away as possible, and finally Melody couldn't take the silence any longer.

"Are you mad at me?"

Jessie looked at her and Melody was a little relieved

to see that she looked confused at this question. Not mad, then – something else. Pained?

"No, I'm not mad," Jessie said, though her tone was still clipped.

"Should I not have tried to kiss you?" Melody asked when it became clear that Jessie wasn't going to offer any more explanation without being prompted. Jessie's eyes darted to the studio door at the word 'kiss,' and Melody knew that the class was about to let out. She'd heard that cool-down song a half dozen times this week alone, and there were only a few seconds left.

She watched Jessie's face twist into a mask of anguish for a moment, her lower lip quivering slightly, and it was hard not to fly out from behind the reception desk and try to comfort her.

"I can't be around you," she said, finally meeting Melody's eyes. The music cut off and the studio erupted into activity as the dancers gathered their things and their parents ushered them toward the door. Just before it opened, Jessie said, "I'm married."

Melody's mouth dropped open and then the lobby filled with chattering kids and goal-oriented parents, everyone colliding in the small space as they tried to find room to put on street shoes and get out of there. Melody couldn't tear her eyes off of Jessie, and Jessie stared straight back at her for a moment. Melody tried to read into that look, to figure out what her words meant for the two of them.

Then Ellie came tearing out of the studio and threw herself into her mother's arms. Jessie looked away first and Melody watched her expression. It took her a second too long to wipe away the anguish and turn it into a smile for Ellie, but then she was right back in her role as the devoted mother, and Melody could practically see the moment she ceased to exist in Jessie's world.

JESSIE WAS true to her word and Melody didn't see much of her for the next few months. She'd come in with Ellie, carefully avoiding Melody's gaze as she signed her into class, and then she would either go directly into the studio with her or she'd dash off to run another errand while Ellie was occupied. When class ended, the two of them would walk out of the studio and immediately head for the door. Ellie still gave Melody a hug when she saw her and waved goodbye on her way out, but Jessie seemed to be doing her best to pretend Melody wasn't even there.

The next time they spoke was at Mary Beth's school-wide Halloween party.

Melody had been drafted to participate in trunk-or-treat for the younger kids and she stood in the frigid air of the parking lot along with about a dozen parents and a couple of the dance instructors. She borrowed her dad's car again and with Andy's help they filled the trunk with plastic skeletons in tutus and big pipe cleaner spiders wearing eight cardboard tap shoes each.

"I'm telling you, this scene would be so much creepier if we made some of that corn syrup Hollywood blood and threw it all over the exterior of the car," Andy said as Melody hot-glued tulle around the hip bones of a skeleton. "All that gore on a white car, it would look so realistic."

"I don't think realistic blood and five-year-old ballerinas are a good mix," Melody said. Then she thought for a minute and said, "Okay, alternative option. The outside of the trunk looks perfectly normal, no fake blood, but we paint the Pavlova logo on it. When you get close to the car, a ballerina pops out from under the bumper and slices your Achilles' tendon, then the trunk pops open and the director of the dance program jumps out and asks you to pack your bags."

"You're right," Andy said. "That's far more appropriate for an audience of kids."

"Just keep gluing tap shoes to those spiders," she told him.

Melody's trunk turned out to be one of the least impressive. As she stood in front of it with a bucket full of candy and kids dashed up and down the line of cars, she looked at the others and tried to guess how much time and money had gone into each of them. Some of the dance moms had built complete worlds in their trunks, dioramas with educational and interactive elements. Certainly more than a couple of stoned teenagers could muster, in any case.

For the first half hour or so, Melody dutifully passed out candy from the bucket that Mary Beth provided, commenting on the kids' costumes and trying not to look for Jessie and Ellie.

Mary Beth, dressed in a mime costume with her

face painted white, came by a few times to refill everyone's buckets, and on her second pass she stopped at Melody's trunk. "That's very clever. Did I tell you that?"

"No," Melody said, scooping fun-sized candy bars into her bucket from Mary Beth's supply. "I'm afraid I'm not winning any awards if it comes down to a competition between me and the moms, though."

"I wouldn't worry about that," Mary Beth said, and she stood beside Melody for a minute or two, watching the chaos around them. There was no one currently at Melody's trunk (they were all occupied with the carnival games and prizes to be won in the other trunks), and after a minute Mary Beth said, "Can I ask you a question, dear?"

"Sure," Melody said.

"What do you think about teaching?"

"Umm, it's a dirty job but somebody's got to do it?" Melody asked, wary of the direction this conversation was taking.

Mary Beth laughed, then said, "No kiddo, I meant you, specifically. What would you say if I asked you to teach a class or two? I've got a lot on my plate and it would be a tremendous help."

"Oh-" Melody said, her heart rate skyrocketing and her hands clenching around the handle of her candy bucket.

"Before you say no," Mary Beth cut in, "Please take some time to think it over. It could be a great career path given your background, and I bet there are a lot of people in Lisbon who would love to have their children trained by a Pavlova dancer."

"*Former* Pavlova dancer," Melody corrected. "I'm afraid my dancing days are over. Besides, I'm not a teacher."

"I could mentor you," Mary Beth insisted. "I know I hired you as the front desk girl, and you've done a truly remarkable job of organizing everything up there. But I can tell you're capable of a whole lot more. What if I arrange for you to just teach one class and see how it goes? I know just the student-"

"No," Melody said, feeling a lump forming in the back of her throat and her hands going shaky at the idea. The thought of stepping foot in a dance studio was enough to send her into a panic attack, and it was the exact thing she'd wanted desperately to avoid when she took this job. "No, Mary Beth. That's not what I signed up for."

Fortunately, a butterfly and a bumble bee came over to Melody's trunk with their pillow cases extended for candy, and Mary Beth wandered away. After the kids left with their bags slightly heavier, Melody leaned against the bumper and put her fingers to her throat to feel her pulse. Her heart was pounding and she felt a little dizzy at the idea of being forced into a studio. She'd have to put her ballet slippers on, and a leotard, and the thought alone made her want to be sick.

After a few minutes, during which time everyone mercifully avoided the inadequately decorated trunk and the green-looking girl leaning against it, Melody felt her heart rate level out and she started to feel better. She'd stood her ground, and hopefully the idea of teaching would never come up again.

"Miss Melody!"

She heard her name being shrieked across the parking lot and knew that Jessie and Ellie had arrived. Ellie came running and threw herself into Melody, wrapping her arms around her hips. Melody saw Jessie from across the parking lot, coming slowly after her daughter, and Melody's pulse quickened. Then Ellie broke the embrace and stood back so that Melody could look at her costume. "Guess what I am!"

Melody had to tear her eyes off of Jessie.

Ellie was wearing an oversized white sweater with little glittery pom-poms sewn all over it along with a pair of tan leggings, and a large red ball made of Styrofoam was tied to her ponytail.

"Hmm," Melody said, glancing over to Jessie for help. She gave none, though, so Melody asked, "Are you a polka dot monster?"

"What? No!" Ellie said incredulously. "I'm an ice cream cone! Look, these are my sprinkles."

She pointed to the pom-poms and Melody threw her hands up. "Of course! I don't know how I missed it."

"In all fairness, her mom's not the greatest seamstress in the world," Jessie said bashfully.

"Better than I could do," Melody said, pointing to her sparse trunk. She didn't want to show it, but she was relieved that Jessie was talking to her – after her admission in the lobby, Melody wasn't sure what to expect. She lowered her bucket of candy so that Ellie could reach it and said with a wink, "You better take a few extra pieces, Little Miss Ice Cream."

"Thanks!" Ellie said, shoving her hand into the bucket, and then she skipped over to the next trunk in the line.

Melody expected Jessie to follow her daughter, probably without another word to her, but instead she lingered in front of Melody's trunk, inspecting the skeleton in its tutu. She said, "That's pretty creative."

"Only if you haven't seen any of the other cars yet," Melody said. "Some of these moms are like professional set designers."

"You don't have to tell me," Jessie answered with a roll of her eyes. "On our way in, I saw a velociraptor whose costume would have put the *Jurassic Park* special effects guy to shame."

Melody laughed and Jessie joined her, eyes flashing over to where Ellie was playing a modified game of Skee-Ball in someone's trunk.

"It's pretty clear that neither of us took this event serious enough," Melody said. "Next year I should let my friend Andy go all out and cover the car in Hollywood blood like he wanted to."

"Honestly, I'm probably going to put in the same amount of effort again next year," Jessie said with a shrug. She was watching as Ellie sank her ball in one of the Skee-Ball cups, her eyes lighting up. "Look how happy she is being a half-assed ice cream cone."

"Oh, who am I kidding?" Melody said with a snort.

"The Mom of the Year over there will probably have a functioning carousel in her trunk by next year, so it's not like I'll ever be able to top that."

"Why would you want to?" Jessie asked. It felt good to have a conversation with her again – Melody was starting to worry that she'd scared her off and they'd be doomed to clipped, curt conversations over the reception desk forever.

"Well, it *is* part of my job," Melody said. "Although I didn't realize trunk-or-treat was included in my job duties when I took the receptionist position."

"Excuse me for saying so," Jessie said a bit tentatively, then soldiered on, "But don't you want more than that?"

Melody felt her pulse quickening again. What was going on with everyone today? She was half-expecting her father to pop out of the nearest trunk next and give her an earful about not fulfilling her potential.

"What's that supposed to mean?" Melody asked, trying not to let too much of an edge creep into her voice.

"I just meant that this seems like a pretty temporary kind of gig," Jessie said. "Part time, not many hours. I figured you were working here while you go to college or something."

"Nope," Melody said sharply. "This is my life."

For a minute or two, they stood together watching Ellie bounce ecstatically from trunk to trunk, the silence between them growing a little uncomfortable. Then Jessie asked, "But why?"

"Why what?"

"Melody, I know that I don't know you very well, or

at all for that matter, but I could tell the minute I met you that you're smart," Jessie said, and Melody couldn't help being at least a little flattered by this. "Why are you content with some part-time gig with no responsibility when anyone who has eyes can see you're capable of so much more? Why *don't* you go to college?"

"Jesus, I knew this was my dad's car, but I didn't realize I was talking to him, too," Melody said. It wasn't fair, and it certainly wasn't how she wanted to talk to Jessie after such a long period of silence between them. But she was on edge from her conversation with Mary Beth and it was too hard to hold back. "Why don't *you* go to college?"

"Melody, I have a five-year-old daughter, two jobs, and half a GED," Jessie said. "Even if I was eligible, I couldn't afford it and I wouldn't have the time for it. What's holding *you* back?"

"I spent the first eighteen years of my life eating, sleeping, and breathing ballet," Melody said. "I'm not built for anything else. At least for now, I have no choice but to work the desk here."

"No choice?" Jessie asked, and she nearly spat the words in her surprise at them. "Waste away here for five years and then tell me how few options you've got."

"Thanks, dad, I'll keep that in mind," Melody said with a roll of her eyes. She had no idea why everyone had decided to gang up on her today, but she was just about done with it.

"Do you know what it's really like to have no options?" Jessie asked. All the fire in her voice was drained away now and she said calmly as she looked into Melody's eyes, "Try being sixteen years old and having to sit on the floor of your classroom because you just realized your belly no longer fits behind a desk. Try going to the office and to tell them you're dropping out, hoping the whole way there that they'll convince you to stay and help you figure out how to work your school schedule around morning sickness and prenatal appointments. And then when you get there, you realize they're secretly thrilled that you and your big belly are finally going to stop darkening their doorways because all they see you as is a bad influence on the other kids. Try going home after that and crying because you made one stupid mistake that ruined every plan you had for your life. *That* is what having no options looks like. Wake up, Melody."

Then she walked away across the asphalt, looking for her daughter, and Melody gave the back tire of her dad's car a swift kick, her candy bucket almost spilling in the process.

CHAPTER FOURTEEN

JESSIE

Jessie was in the middle of a long and tedious shift at the grocery store and there weren't many customers in the store at the moment. The managers always hated to see cashiers standing around doing nothing, or worse – talking to each other – so usually she tried to keep herself busy during these lulls. It was a crime to enjoy yourself at work, or so the management staff believed.

She had already straightened all the magazines, and then the candy bars and the refrigerator full of soda at the end of her register. All of it took no more than fifteen minutes, during which time a few customers trickled into the store but none came to check out. Lisbon was a town of about thirty thousand people, most of them school-aged or employed during the day, and very few of them found reason to go to the store at one in the afternoon on a Tuesday. It made for long shifts sometimes.

Jessie sighed with boredom. Her feet hurt and the

padded floor mat did very little to lessen the ache of being on her feet up to sixteen hours a day between her two jobs.

She turned her attention to tidying up the space behind the register, where plastic clothes hangers tended to get tangled and spare rolls of register tape were haphazardly stacked. Jessie began to take everything out of the cubby hole beneath the register to organize it, and behind the register tape she found a tattered paperback book.

Pulling it out, Jessie stifled a laugh at the cover, a cheesy romance bearing all the trappings of cliché – the long-haired, bare-chested man. The damsel with heaving breasts who clung to him. The horse. Jessie ran her fingers over the raised letters of the cringeworthy title – *Master of Desire* – and then with a roll of her eyes she chucked it on top of the register to finish her cleaning job. Some other cashier must have brought the book with her to sneak pages from it between customers, stashed it at the back of the cubby and forgotten about it.

Jessie tidied up the whole area, her eyes going back to the book again and again. She was sure it would be awful, like all cheesy romances were. She helped a customer or two, checked the time, and then there was nothing left to do. With a sigh and a quick glance around to make sure there were no managers nearby, she reluctantly picked up the book. It was better than staring at the clock, and she was a *little* curious about these romance rags that every other woman on the planet seemed to be obsessed with. What could be so great about a contrived love story between such stereotypical characters?

She flipped the book open to a random page near the beginning and began reading, ready to hate it. The next time she looked up from the book's pages, though, a cashier was standing impatiently in front of her.

"Huh?" Jessie said, feeling a little disoriented as she realized how absorbed she'd become in the book.

"I said I'm here to relieve you," the cashier said with a roll of his eyes. "Your shift's over."

Jessie looked at the clock and was surprised to find that it was already three minutes past five. "Oh, okay. Thanks."

She looked at the book and thought about shoving it behind the register tapes again, but she'd become invested in the characters, and the last ten pages had been real nail-biters with the tension between the hero and heroine building to a fever pitch. Jessie slipped her thumb into the book to hold her place and then held it behind her back in what she hoped was an inconspicuous move as she squeezed past the cashier and went to clock out.

She had an hour before she had to be at the diner and Steve and Ellie were expecting her to come home for dinner in between like she usually did. But the moment Jessie climbed into her car at the back of the darkened parking lot, she opened the book again, tilting it toward the streetlamp nearby to read. Jessie didn't know what had gotten into her – she always used to detest anything with a remotely romantic element, but she couldn't just stop reading in the middle of the scene.

The hero – a Master-at-Arms in the Navy – had just learned that he was shipping out in the morning to a dangerous war that he likely wouldn't come back from, and he was on his way to say goodbye to the woman he loved but who he was too pragmatic to marry. He didn't want to leave her a widow, but he had to at least give her a suitable goodbye. She was a proper, chaste young lady, but they let passion win and fell into bed together.

Jessie could feel her pulse quicken as the pace of the scene sped up and the characters' clothes fell away. She imagined the hero transforming into a woman as the Master-at-Arms' hands played over the heroine's bodice, and then she imagined the two characters becoming herself and Melody. Heat rose into her face, among other places, and she knew she shouldn't be thinking like that but it was too late. She'd fallen into the pages of the book again and the rest of the world melted away.

The hero – Jessie – was trying to resist the heroine's advances, telling her that it was a mistake to be together like this because it would only make the pain so much more exquisite were they to be separated by the ravages of war. The heroine – Melody – would abide by no objections, though, and she took the hero by the hand, pulling her into the bedroom.

The hero unlaced the bodice of the heroine's dress, and then put her hand on her bare chest, tracing her fingers down her sternum and then over the soft flesh of her breast, and Jessie felt a jolt of pleasure course through her as her breath hitched.

She glanced around the parking lot, but there wasn't a single car nearby and she was free to lose herself in this explicit fantasy. Her eyes scanned the words quickly and her pulse pounded in her ears.

The heroine continued to trace the hero's hand down her stomach, and then she pressed her fingers between her thighs. The hero bit her lip as they both let out a low moan of desire, and then she pushed the heroine down on the bed, crawling in to meet her and bringing her fingers back to seek out that warm, deliciously wet place. The heroine's back arched against the mattress and she reached for the hero, clinging to her in her ecstasy.

Heart pounding in her chest, Jessie unbuttoned her khakis and thrust one hand beneath the waistband, stroking her clit to the rhythm of the scene.

The heroine wrapped her body around the hero, her thighs clinging to Jessie as her hand continued to slide up and down over her and elicit cry after cry of pleasure. Just as she felt the heroine reaching the point of no return, the hero withdrew her hand and swung her leg over the heroine's hips, straddling her and bending down to kiss the impossibly soft flesh of her lips just as she penetrated her with two fingers. The heroine turned her face to the pillow, an exquisite agony playing out across her face as she cried out and bucked her hips against the hero's hand, and as the heroine climaxed, so did Jessie.

Panting, she doubled over toward the steering wheel,

her body contracting around her fingers, and the book falling into the foot well beneath her.

"Oh my god," she whispered after a few moments spent composing herself and catching her breath.

In her whole life she'd never orgasmed that hard, nor had she ever been so helpless to pursue her desires, and as she buttoned her pants a strong sense of guilt washed over her. She should be home with her daughter and husband, not thinking about Melody like this. Jessie retrieved the worn paperback, tossing it onto the seat beside her with the intention of putting it back where she found it as soon as possible.

That had been a desperate moment, but she had to admit it felt good to let herself explore the idea of Melody, even if it was only in her head.

JESSIE DIDN'T KEEP her promise to herself about returning *Master of Desire* – at least not right away. She kept the book for two more days, long enough to finish the story and commit a few impactful scenes to memory, altering the pronouns and characters to fit her preferences. By the time she closed the back cover and the hero and heroine walked away into the sunset, they had completely ceased to be the military man and his damsel in distress. They were Jessie and Melody, transplanted to war-torn eighteenth century America.

She had a hard time putting the book back because of that. It was an awfully cliché romance, but it had become hers in a way that no romantic film had ever captured love for her before. Usually, they just made her feel a little sick to her stomach because of how impossible they were to relate to – the last romantic movie she'd seen was *The Notebook,* which her best friend, Blaire, brought over on a day when Jessie was having a particularly bad bout of morning sickness and couldn't get out of bed.

She was engaged to Steve by then, and becoming aware of her attraction to women, and she ran from the room to be sick during the climax scene in the movie. Blaire blamed it on the pregnancy, which probably didn't help, but it was more than that. Jessie felt so hollow when she watched that love story unfold. She already knew that a life with Steve meant she'd never get to know what it felt like to be so passionately in love.

Jessie took the book to her next shift at the grocery store, telling herself she'd tuck it away beneath the register, but it came home again with her in the oversized pocket of her ugly blue vest. It seemed like a tragedy to give it away – it was like giving away the version of Melody and herself that she'd created within its pages. What if they *only* existed within the pages of that book?

She kept it almost a week, and she felt ridiculous carrying the tattered paperback around, constantly afraid that someone would see the cheesy Fabio-on-a-horse cover and judge her for it, or worse – Steve might find it. But if she didn't have the book, then all she had was a passionless marriage built around assuring the financial security of her daughter.

Then one day it occurred to her that there was a

better way to get what she needed than pretending that the Fabio-type hero was a girl. On her lunch break, she went online in search of books whose characters matched the ones in her mind a bit better – ones that didn't require quite so much gender-bending – so that she could finally put *Master of Desire* back into its hiding place behind the register tape.

Jessie's heart was pounding as she typed the words 'lesbian romance novels' into the search engine, the first and only time she'd been explicit about her sexuality, and a couple thousand results came up. Jessie spent most of her fifteen-minute break reading synopses, hoping to find the perfect book to stand as a proxy for all the things her heart ached to do with Melody. In the end, she settled on a couple of promising novels and then she had to go back to her register.

The store had a pretty strict 'no cellphones' rule to go along with its other 'no fun' rules, and Jessie was forced to leave hers – and thus, the novels - in her locker. That was one benefit of the paperback – easier to disguise, easier to pretend it had been left behind by a customer.

Waiting out the last three hours of her shift turned out to be almost unbearable as Jessie wondered what was waiting for her in those lesbian romance novels. If *Master of Desire* had done so much for her, then these books must be even better.

Every time Jessie thought about them, her heart began beating a little faster. As much as she wanted to indulge her fantasies and explore a part of herself that had been closed off for so long, what she was doing felt wrong. She'd put so much effort into hiding *Master of Desire* from Steve, and even though she hadn't consciously thought about it while she was downloading the books to her phone, it had occurred to her that it would be a lot easier to hide an ebook from her husband than a paperback. She knew he'd be upset if he saw what she was reading.

Steve was no bigot, but having a lesbian for a wife was bound to put strain on their relationship. Jessie knew from the moment that she found out she was pregnant that she and Steve would never be compatible, but because her ultimate goal was just to make Ellie's life a happy one, it hadn't seemed worth announcing her sexuality to the world. It had become a moot point the moment she accepted Steve's proposal in the name of making a good life for her daughter.

Steve knew the level of intimacy in their relationship was almost at zero, of course, but in their five and a half years of marriage, he'd never guessed the reason. Jessie figured it was hard to see something when you didn't have time to pay attention to it, and even harder when you didn't want to see it.

She had no idea what effect it would have on their marriage if she were to come out about her sexuality now that she was beginning to explore it. Continuing to stay in a relationship with someone who would never want him back would be a tough conversation to have with Steve. She hoped he would see it from her perspective – it was all for Ellie, every decision she made up til now was for Ellie – but this was so far beyond the scope of any problems they'd had in the past, Jessie didn't know what to expect.

The best thing would be for her to continue keeping the secret. If Melody had awoken something inside her that couldn't be ignored, then the best she could do was relegate that part of her to fantasies that she kept hidden away from the rest of the world.

CHAPTER FIFTEEN

MELODY

Melody sat on a bench in the locker room while a
dozen other dancers moved around her. They
became a blur of tulle and silk, and Melody was feeling a
little dizzy. She'd been sick all week, a stomach bug that
seemed to work through everyone else in a day or two but
which lingered in her. It didn't matter how feverish she
felt, though. Missing this audition wasn't an option.

Neither was missing class, or her scheduled time in
the practice studio, or her academic classes.

Melody threw up and then pressed a cold compress to
her forehead in the dorm bathroom before dragging herself
across campus to the auditorium this morning. She still
felt a little sick to her stomach as she laced up her pointe
shoes, and her fingers felt fat and clumsy. This was the last
audition before Christmas break, the last opportunity to
get out of the chorus and prove that she deserved to be here
and all her time and effort, as well as and her parents'
money, was well-spent.

After she stuffed her blistered, sore toes into her shoes, Melody still had about ten minutes before her call time. She should use it to warm up, to stretch and practice her routine one more time, but all she could do was lean against the cool metal of the lockers and watch a few dozen girls bustle back and forth, getting ready to dance or packing up after their auditions.

None of them seemed half as concerned with the outcome as she was, and none of them was this sick.

Melody pressed her fingers to her cheeks, trying to derive a little coolness from them, and the sound of classical music filtered in from the stage. She felt her pulse quicken and something hot rose in the back of her throat. There were only two auditions ahead of her, and another bout of sickness seemed imminent.

"Melody Bledsoe?"

She turned her head, following her name. There was a woman standing in the open door with a clipboard tucked into her elbow, and Melody thought she looked wavy somehow, not entirely real. Or maybe it was just the fever.

"Melody?" The woman called again, and Melody raised her hand limply.

"I'm here."

"You're up next," the woman said, checking something off on her clipboard. "Come to the stage now, please."

"I'll be right there," Melody said, and then she watched the woman float through the door. It swung shut, and suddenly she felt very alone in this room full of people. Something lurched in her stomach and she dragged herself up off the bench.

Walking proved difficult. Her vision continued to be distorted and the locker room she'd become so familiar with in the last four months suddenly looked almost unrecognizable. With a great deal of effort, Melody found her way to the back of the locker room, and though she'd been looking for the toilet stalls, she found the showers instead. She went into the first one, drawing the curtain shut and allowing herself to collapse against the cool tile wall.

She just needed to cool off and she wanted to sit down, just for a moment before her audition. It felt like she was in an inferno even though her cheek rested against the cool shower tile, and in her half-delirious state, her hand found the cold water knob. She jumped as the water hit her face, icy and soothing as it soaked her leotard and ran into her pointe shoes, and as her legs gave out and she slid down the wall, her wrist caught on something sharp.

"Ouch!" She hissed, white-hot pain shooting up her arm as she slumped to the floor. She looked down and saw a bright red river flowing from her forearm and swirling down the drain.

She looked up and saw the culprit, an old metal soap dish affixed to the wall and broken off at an odd angle. Her arm caught on the jagged edge, slicing open as she slid down the wall.

Melody looked back down at her wrist. It was alarming how much blood there was, and how calm she felt about it. She reflected curiously on the fact that her stomach didn't hurt anymore, now that her body found something more important to focus on. The last thing she remembered was the pleasant realization that she would miss her audition, and she would never need to know whether she was a failure. She closed her eyes and let the cold water run over the open wound on her forearm.

CHAPTER SIXTEEN

MELODY

"Why don't we talk about New York today?"

Dr. Riley was sitting in her customary position, chair turned toward Melody with her notepad in her lap, and Melody had been sitting pensively for the first ten minutes of the session. She'd been grumpy about work ever since Mary Beth and Jessie ganged up on her at the Halloween party, and she didn't feel much like talking.

This was a mistake – Melody had learned pretty early on in her sessions with Dr. Riley that it was best to fill the silence with anything she could think of until the hour was up. If she did all the talking, she could direct the session and steer clear of topics she wasn't comfortable with. They'd only talked directly about New York once before, in her very first session, and even then it had been as brief and factual as Melody could make it.

"I'd rather not," she said. "Can we talk about the fact that my kid sister doesn't go a single day without needling me about the fact that I'm a failure who had to move back in with her parents?"

"Is this Starla's session?" Dr. Riley asked, a little more sarcastically than was warranted, Melody thought.

"No."

"Let's talk about your breakdown," Dr. Riley said abruptly, and Melody saw her pen dip toward her notepad. She knew Melody hated it when she took notes, like she was an animal being studied, but she also knew Dr. Riley had been itching to get around to this subject for a while. This was what Melody's parents were paying her for, after all.

"What do you want to know?" She asked with a sigh, crossing her arms in front of her chest to make it clear that any information she gave would be extracted under duress.

"Tell me what you were thinking just before your end-of-semester audition," Dr. Riley said, "in the locker room just before you were supposed to go on stage."

"I was thinking that I might throw up," Melody said.

They'd talked about this before. Dr. Riley knew she had the flu and that she'd collapsed in the shower. She knew even better than Melody that the stage assistant found her unconscious and bloody and that she'd been taken by ambulance to the hospital, where they put her on a seventy-two-hour watch because everyone assumed she was suicidal. Melody's mother had filled Dr. Riley in on all of those details because Melody herself had no memory of it. All she had for a souvenir was a jagged pink scar running down her forearm – oh, and six months in therapy.

"What about the idea of going on stage made you feel sick to your stomach?" Dr. Riley asked.

"It wasn't the audition," Melody said testily. "I had a stomach bug."

"Are you sure?"

"Of course I'm sure," Melody snapped. "I was throwing up for over a week."

"The doctor in the emergency room noted in your chart that there were no physical symptoms to indicate illness," Dr. Riley said delicately. This wasn't the first time Melody heard that. When her parents drove to New York to pick her up from the hospital, they questioned her at length about why she would cut herself like that, and they believed every word the ER doctor said, taking it as damning evidence of her desperation.

"Maybe I got it out of my system by then," Melody said, raising her voice a little higher than necessary as she tugged her sleeves down over her wrists. She did it whenever she thought about the end of her dance career, or felt self-conscious about the scar. Dr. Riley let the silence stretch out between them for a moment or two – she was manipulative when she needed to be, and even though she let Melody spend the hour talking about nonsense most of the time, Melody could never completely let down her guard in case of moments like this.

"You know, anxiety can be a pretty tricky thing to deal with," Dr. Riley said delicately. "The fear reaction can elicit any number of mental or physical symptoms in an effort to activate the fight-or-flight response and keep you out of danger."

Melody looked up at Dr. Riley, whose pen was still poised over the blank legal pad, waiting for a breakthrough. "What are you trying to say?"

"Just that you had an awful lot on your shoulders at Pavlova, and most strains of the stomach flu don't linger for several weeks," Dr. Riley said, choosing her words carefully. Melody kept her arms crossed as she listened. "Think about how your body felt when you were in that shower stall. You described nausea, dizziness and fever, but you also described visual disturbances and a racing pulse – those are all symptoms of an extreme panic reaction. Melody, isn't it possible that you saw that broken soap dish as an escape from the humiliation of failing as a dancer?"

"I don't want to talk about this," Melody said. "Can we change the subject?"

"Does it make you uncomfortable to consider that possibility?" Dr. Riley pressed. "The possibility that what happened in the shower was intentional?"

"Fuck you," Melody hissed. "You're supposed to be the one person who's on my side about that, who's supposed to take my word for it."

"Melody, injuries like that don't just happen on accident."

"Were you there?" Melody asked, her voice rising into a shrieking register. "Because I was there the whole fucking time, watching myself fall farther and farther behind the rest of the class no matter how much time I put in practicing. No matter what I did I was at the bottom of my class and nothing I did was good enough. My turn-out wasn't good enough, my balance wasn't good enough, my techniques weren't advanced enough. I was the small-town girl who thought she was going to take New York by storm, except the only thing I was doing was wasting everyone's time and putting my whole family deeper and deeper into debt for every day that I stayed."

"How do you know you were wasting everyone's time?" Dr. Riley asked gently. "You were accepted into a very prestigious program, chosen out of hundreds of applicants. Why do you think you were destined to fail?"

"Not everyone who gets accepted succeeds," Melody said. "Just because I studied at Pavlova didn't mean I'd ever get a job as anything other than a mediocre chorus dancer at the back of the stage, just like I was in the school performances. If no one ever saw me and they didn't even realize I was there, then I *was* wasting everyone's time."

"And your parents' money," Dr. Riley said, and Melody shot her a glare for so helpfully bringing that aspect to the forefront.

"Yes."

"That must have been a lot of pressure to handle," Dr. Riley said. "Especially as a new adult, living in such a big city so far away from your family and friends."

"Yeah," Melody said, hanging her head and watching as a tear fell from the corner of her eye and stained the thigh of her jeans a darker color. The wet spot bloomed outward for a second, and then she said quietly, almost imperceptibly, "No one ever quits Pavlova because they can't take the pressure."

Dr. Riley didn't try to respond to this, and after a moment Melody inhaled sharply, putting her head back to stare at the ceiling and try to ward off more tears. She said to the ceiling, "Everyone just assumes that when you reach that level, you're already made of stone and nothing can touch you because you've already become what they all expect."

"And what's that?"

"A prima," Melody said, her lip curling up a little bit as she looked at Dr. Riley finally. "A principle dancer. The best of the best. The only honorable way out is to be so physically beaten down that you can't continue. I knew a dancer who did an entire show on a broken toe, and girls with stress fractures in their shins, and they all just kept dancing. Dr. Riley, I didn't slice my forearm open on purpose, but when I woke up in the hospital and the doctor asked me why I tried to kill myself, I didn't correct him because I knew it was a way out."

The tears were streaming down her face now, and she tried to flick them away with her hands but it did no good. They came so heavily it almost felt like being in the shower again.

Dr. Riley reached over and handed her a box of tissues and then waited patiently. When Melody finally got herself under control again, she said, "Good. Now we can really get to work."

"H'LO?" Melody grumbled the word, her brain still swimming out of sleep as she answered her phone through muscle memory alone. It was early on Saturday morning, and when she glanced at the time she saw it was not quite eight a.m.

"Kiddo, I need a favor!" The voice on the other end of the line was a little hoarse but unmistakably Mary Beth.

"What's wrong?" Melody asked, sitting up and trying to wipe the sleep from her eyes.

"I'm contagious," Mary Beth said. "I woke up this morning and my tonsils were swollen to the size of apples. Saw the doctor already and he said I have strep throat. I got Emily to cover my other classes today, but I need you to teach beginner ballet."

"What? No," Melody started to object, but Mary Beth interrupted.

"Please," she said, the froggy nature of her voice emphasized as she put strain on it. "I wouldn't ask if there were any other options."

Melody rolled her eyes. She very much doubted that, especially after the conversation they'd had at the Halloween party. She wondered just how sick Mary Beth really was. "I really don't think I can. I'm not trained as a teacher."

"That's ridiculous," Mary Beth said. "If you're good enough to get into Pavlova, I think you can figure out how to teach a few five-year-olds how to plié."

Melody imagined herself putting on her leotard and

ballet slippers, anxiety rising in her throat, and then she thought about the fact that Ellie Cartwright was in that class. Jessie would be sitting there the whole time, along with a row of other dance moms all holding notepads and staring at her and taking notes on the recital routine. Melody didn't want to set foot in the studio, and feeling like she was in a fishbowl with all those eyes on her would be bad enough if a pair of those eyes weren't Jessie's mossy green ones.

"I can't," Melody said.

"You have to," Mary Beth said. "I'm too contagious."

And then before Melody had a chance to object again, Mary Beth hung up.

"Seriously?" Melody quipped to her empty bedroom.

She didn't have a whole lot of choice, though – either she taught the class or she would have to call everyone in it and tell them the class was cancelled. The idea certainly crossed her mind to do just that, but when she got out of bed, she went over to her dresser and pulled out a neatly folded and long-forgotten leotard from the bottom drawer. She laid it out on her bed, then she dug an old warm-up sweater with long sleeves out of the back of her closet and laid that down beside the leotard.

Melody spent the morning trying to distract herself from what was coming in the afternoon. She went over to Andy's before work and chattered nervously to him about how Mary Beth had forced her into teaching the class, but when he nudged the bong toward her she waved it away and said she needed to get to work. At the reception desk, she did her best to stay busy and keep her mind occupied.

In the back of her mind, though, she was running through the playlist of music she always heard Mary Beth using for the beginner ballet class. She also thought about the choreography for their recital dance, wondering how closely she'd guessed it – Mary Beth wouldn't expect her to rehearse that with them, but it would make the class go faster if she did.

When twelve forty-five rolled around, she got up from the desk and went into the bathroom down the hall to change into her leotard and ballet slippers. It was the first time she'd worn any of it since coming home from New York, and the way the spandex hugged her like a second skin felt uncomfortably familiar. She pulled the soft pink sweater on over the leotard, tugging the sleeves down to her wrists, then slid into an old pair of ballet slippers. She had to admit it was nice putting them on without the shooting pain associated with blistered toes and so many hours of practice.

She heard the front door open and little ballerinas began to pour into the lobby. Melody put her hand on the bathroom door and took a long, deep breath, then went out to meet them.

"Miss Melody!" Ellie was the first spot her, and she made it about halfway down the hall toward her when she stopped, spotting Melody's wardrobe change, then said, "Hey, you're dressed up like a ballerina."

"Yep," Melody said, glancing over Ellie's head at her mother waiting down the hall. Jessie was staring at her in the leotard, and even though she'd worn something like it every day for an entire semester at Pavlova, suddenly Melody felt indecent.

"Why?" Ellie demanded as Melody led her toward the studio.

"Well, it looks like I'm going to be teaching your class today," Melody said. "Why don't you go in and take a spot on the floor? I'll be right in."

She dodged into the safety behind the reception desk, not quite ready to set foot in the studio, and watched as the rest of the dancers entered the studio. Jessie lingered behind for just a moment, approaching the desk.

"You look good," she said, color coming into her cheeks. "Very professional."

"Oh shut up," Melody said with a smirk. She was actually grateful that Jessie was standing here distracting her from the way her pulse was beginning to race and pound in her ears. If she was alone at the desk, Melody worried it might start to feel too much like the locker room at her last audition.

"I'm sorry about our last conversation," Jessie said. "I was out of line."

"It's okay," Melody said. Jessie seemed to be leaning just slightly too far over the ledge of the reception counter, the space between them closing in. Melody was suddenly feeling bashful, so she looked down at her leotard and added, "Just don't get the impression by this that you were right or anything."

Jessie laughed, then Melody took another deep breath and finally felt ready to come out from behind the desk. Even if she wasn't ready, there was no more time to delay – she needed to start the class. Jessie went into the studio and found a chair along the wall with the other moms, and Melody followed her. As she stepped over the threshold, the leather soles of her slippers gripped the waxed wood floor just like they always had before.

"Hi everyone," she said as she walked over to the sound system mounted on one wall. She felt heat rising into her cheeks as a momentary panic washed over her again, everything Jessie had done to distract her in the lobby dissipating as she realized that this was the first time she'd set foot in a studio since she left New York. Melody kept her face turned away from everyone, trying to hide the color in her cheeks, as she queued the warm-up music that Mary Beth always used.

It took her a minute to figure out the stereo, and when she finally turned around, she saw almost two dozen little ballerinas looking expectantly up from the floor at her, as well as about a dozen parents.

"I hope you all recognize me from the front desk," she said. "I'm Melody, and I'm going to be filling in for Mary Beth today because she's feeling under the weather."

A dozen wide, expectant eyes followed her every move and her heart pounded as she came to the center of the room and sat down on the floor with the kids. She shot a quick look at Jessie, who was smiling encouragingly, and then she started directing them through a series of warm-up stretches.

After a few minutes, the music started to get into her bones and Melody remembered how good it felt to stretch her muscles out. She relaxed a bit, even managing to lose herself in the moment a few times, and before she knew it, the hour was over. They'd progressed through floor and barre stretches and then to their recital routine. Melody got bold and walked over to Jessie's chair to glance over her shoulders at the notes she'd jotted on her steno pad, and she was pleased with herself when she saw that she hadn't been far off when she guessed at the choreography.

By the time the kids and parents streamed back into the hall, Melody felt downright good, and she was thoroughly surprised at how much she'd enjoyed teaching the class. Of course she wouldn't tell Mary Beth that – the next time she saw her, Melody intended to tell her that it was the most harrowing experience of her life.

"Nice job," Jessie said as she and Ellie passed Melody on the way out of the studio, and for just a second, Melody felt Jessie's hand brush across her back. It could have been a dream.

MARY BETH WAS BACK to work the following day with a heavy dose of antibiotics and her doctor's assurance that she was not contagious after all. Melody thought she still sort of looked like crap, though, her voice raspy and her eyelids drooping with exhaustion.

"I never get sick," Mary Beth croaked as she and Melody walked into the school twenty minutes before the first class of the day. "I think the last time I had a cold was 2007, and the last time I was too sick to come to work – well, I don't think that's ever happened before. When I do get sick, though, it really knocks me on my ass."

Melody could relate – the last time she'd gotten sick, she ended up leaving Pavlova in the back of an ambulance.

"I'm glad you're feeling better," Melody said, although the redness around Mary Beth's nose and the sound of her voice didn't indicate that she was all that much better. Melody tried to casually keep her distance.

"Thanks for covering the beginner ballet class," Mary Beth said. "How did it go?"

"Umm," Melody started, considering her options.

Just for the sheer trickery of being forced to teach the class, she wanted to tell Mary Beth it was awful. She wanted her to feel guilty for making Melody do something that she'd been very clear about not wanting to do.

In reality, though, she actually kind of liked it. The kids were so excited about everything she showed them and it reminded her of how she felt when she was a kid and just learning ballet. It was nice to see it through innocent eyes again, instead of through the lens of judgment, guilt and fear that Melody wore now.

So Melody went back on her promise to herself and decided to be honest. She said, "It was actually not bad."

Mary Beth's eyes lit up, and suddenly she looked at least fifty percent less sick.

"Good," she exclaimed as Melody stepped behind the reception desk. Mary Beth was grinning at her and leaning over the ledge conspiratorially, and then she said,

"That's so good to hear because I have an opportunity for you, kiddo."

"What is it?" Melody asked tentatively.

Anxiety rose in her chest and she wondered when people were going to stop pushing her out of her comfort zone – her parents, Dr. Riley, and now Mary Beth. Wasn't it enough progress for one week that she'd taught the beginner class and it hadn't killed her like she expected it to?

"There's a student who I think would really shine if she had some one-on-one instruction," Mary Beth said.

"You want me to teach a private lesson?" Melody asked, already coming up with her list of reasons why she couldn't do it. She wasn't qualified or experienced enough to teach. She wasn't in shape. She couldn't spare the time between her reception job and the busy social life she had going on in Andy's basement. Her parents would be too pleased about it and mistake it for further progress.

"Yes," Mary Beth said, "a series of them, ideally."

"I can't-"

"You'd be the perfect person to get this young lady up to speed," Mary Beth went on, completely ignoring the fact that Melody had even spoken. "I see a lot of potential in her, and from the feedback I heard from the mothers after yesterday's class, I see potential in you, too."

"Mary Beth, I don't think-"

"Don't say no right now," Mary Beth cut her off. Her voice may have been froggy and hoarse, but she was persistent. "Take the afternoon to think it over before you give me an answer. Of course it would be in addition to your reception duties, and you'd get a stipend for teaching the class. Private lessons pay double."

She said this last bit with a wink, as if money were the only driving factor in whether or not Melody could drag herself back into the studio.

"I have to get ready to teach the tap dancers now," Mary Beth said, heading to the restroom to get dressed. She disappeared down the hall, but a second later she popped her head back into the reception area to say, "Oh, I forgot to mention the student is Ellie Cartwright."

Then she was gone again, and Melody's cheeks were turning red. It couldn't have been a coincidence the way Mary Beth said that – she must have remembered seeing Melody and Jessie together at the recital, or noticed some look they exchanged over the reception desk. Could she really have known that the possibility of spending more time with Jessie would influence her decision to teach Ellie's private lessons? Not that it should matter – Jessie was married and she'd made it clear that nothing could ever happen between them. It did change things, though... at least a little bit.

The front door chimed as it swung open and a couple of dancers arrived for the intermediate tap lesson.

Melody greeted them and got them signed in, and then she sat down behind the reception desk. Maybe she was reading too much into it and Mary Beth had only said what she did because Ellie was always so animated when she came into the studio and never failed to give Melody a hug. She was a sweet girl, but Melody didn't think she was anyone special to her – Ellie gave *everyone* a hug.

She thought about what it would feel like to intentionally enter that dance studio again, and do it on a regular basis. It would probably just be one class a week and it *had* felt good to teach the beginner class. Besides, Mary Beth was right – Ellie had been in that class for all of four lessons before she'd memorized the choreography for last year's recital. Even if it turned out that she wasn't specially gifted, she was determined as hell, and anyone willing to put in that much effort deserved the extra encouragement private lessons could offer.

CHAPTER SEVENTEEN

STEVE

Steve Cartwright was exhausted when he came home after working a double shift at the factory. It was past midnight and both Jessie and Ellie were already asleep. His coveralls were smeared with grease and all he wanted was a shower and his bed.

He kicked off his shoes just inside the door, then peeled off the coveralls, stripping down to his tee shirt and boxers. He always thought it was a cruel thing to do, leaving something this filthy on the coat rack for Jessie to deal with, but she said she'd rather he left his coveralls isolated on the coat rack than find them mixed in with the rest of the laundry.

He pulled the collar of his tee shirt up over his nose and sniffed. There was a faint body odor – fourteen hours in a hot factory would do that – but it wasn't that bad all things considered. It would at least keep for twenty minutes while he had a beer to unwind before hopping in the shower. Or maybe he'd just take the beer into the shower with him – there were very few things as satisfying after a long shift at a grueling job than drinking a cold one while hot water washed away the stink of the day.

Steve went into the kitchen and got a can of Budweiser out of the refrigerator, then walked slowly down the hall, careful to avoid the creaky board about two thirds of the way to Ellie's door. He stepped around it and then quietly opened the door.

Ellie was sound asleep with one leg flung over the edge of the mattress, just like she almost always was when Steve got home from work. In the past month, he probably hadn't seen his daughter awake more than eight times. At least he got the weekends off – Jessie wasn't usually so lucky, juggling shifts between two different jobs. Steve crept across the floor and tucked Ellie back in. She almost always managed to scrunch her sheets down to the foot of the bed in the process of falling asleep, and Steve couldn't help finding it endearing.

He gently lifted her leg back into the bed, then pulled the sheets over her. Now that she was in a dead sleep, she'd stay this way til morning.

"Good night, bug," Steve whispered to her, then tiptoed back out of the room.

He went into the bathroom, where he cracked the beer can open and let the steam from the shower fill the room as he slowly enjoyed his evening brewski, a few hours late tonight. He scrubbed as much grease off his hands as he could, then crumpled the beer can and tossed it into the trash before wrapping a towel around his waist and heading into the bedroom.

Jessie was sleeping heavily, a faint snore coming out of her as her chest rose and fell, and she had one leg draped over the edge of the mattress – like mother, like daughter. The only difference was that Steve had long ago given up on trying to put Jessie into a more comfortable position. No matter how many times he brought her leg back onto the mattress or straightened out her sheets, she always reverted right back to the way she was.

"Jess?" he whispered. Damn it all if he hadn't forgotten what her schedule was tomorrow, and he couldn't leave it til morning or else Ellie might not get to school on time. Jessie didn't stir. Steve went over to his dresser and changed into a pair of pajama pants, then stepped a little closer to her side of the bed and said again, a little louder, "Jess!"

"Mmpfhh," she moaned and rolled away from him.

"Shit," he muttered, and then he saw her phone on the night table beside her.

She always kept her work schedule in her calendar – he could check it without waking her from the sleep that she clearly needed. It was like trying to wake the dead anyway. He pulled the phone off its charger and went over to a small bench in front of the window to try and figure out where the hell her calendar app was.

He unlocked the phone and the screen was filled with text. It looked like Jessie was in the middle of reading a book when she went to bed, and Steve almost closed the window. Then a phrase jumped out at him.

...touched her breasts...

"What have we got here?" He murmured, glancing over at his sleeping wife.

For all the times she failed to show even the slightest interest in him, Steve had no idea Jessie even *had* a sex drive, and here she was reading dirty books! Pushing aside a mild annoyance at the fact that Jessie apparently preferred romance novels to her husband, he read a few lines.

I unlaced the corset as quickly as my fingers could work their way through the laces, the Lady's breath rising and falling rapidly as she waited. The moment the corset fell away, she turned and threw her arms around me, her fingers playing through the long curls of my hair.

"Touch me," I begged, sliding her hand beneath my petticoat.

"Louisa, we can't," the Lady objected, but though her lips protested, her body met mine with a fervor.

"What the fuck?" Steve whispered into the darkened room. He flipped a few pages forward, to the meat of the sex scene, and then glanced again at Jessie. This was a lesbian book.

Confused and unsure what to do with this information, he just sat there. His wife, who most of the time he privately suspected was frigid, was reading about lesbian sex. But what could he do about it? Wake her up and confront her at one in the morning?

After a minute of contemplation, Steve closed the app and found Jessie's calendar, memorizing her schedule for the next few days, and then he walked over to the night table and plugged Jessie's phone back in. He set it down, then thought again and picked it up, opening the book and flipping back to the page he'd found it on.

Then he went around to his side of the bed and spent the next hour staring at the ceiling and wondering what the right response is to something like this rather than getting the sleep he so desperately wanted.

CHAPTER EIGHTEEN

JESSIE

The sun had not yet risen in the sky when Jessie and Ellie climbed into her old rust bucket Sebring and drove over to the dance school for Ellie's first private lesson. The sky was streaked with pink and there weren't even any other drivers on the road yet, but Ellie was practically bouncing in her seat.

"I can't believe I get to do ballet *twice* a week now," she was chattering, meanwhile Jessie reached for the coffee mug in the center console and tried not to yawn too much. She stayed up late the night before, sucked into one of the books she bought the previous week, and now she was having a hard time keeping her eyes open, let alone matching Ellie's level of enthusiasm.

Of course, the early hour was not entirely to blame for this. Part of her hesitance came from the fact that Melody would be Ellie's teacher. Jessie assumed it would be Mary Beth, and she hadn't thought to clarify the matter until after she paid upfront for the first lesson.

"Mommy!"

"What?" Jessie said irritably, wincing at the pitch of her daughter's voice so early in the morning. They were pulling into the parking lot and Jessie saw the white sedan that she recognized from Melody's trunk-or-treat effort a few months before.

"Thank you. I love you," Ellie said, shooting her a huge grin as she unlatched her seatbelt and bolted out of the car.

"Brat," Jessie muttered after Ellie had vacated the vehicle.

Of course she didn't mean it, but Ellie *would* have to say that after she'd gotten snappish with her. Jessie knew how excited she was about private lessons and the possibility of joining the girls she'd met last year in intermediate ballet, and she also knew that it didn't matter *who* was teaching this class, she'd make the sacrifice for her daughter's happiness.

Still, the idea of being alone in the studio with Melody – alone in the whole school, for that matter – made Jessie's stomach a little jumpy. It seemed almost inevitable that at some point in the next hour, she'd find herself alone with Melody. It wasn't like anything could happen between them if that was the case, but Jessie didn't think she could stand the tension.

"Mommy, come on," Ellie called from the door.

"Just a minute, bug," Jessie said, turning around in her seat to find the little dog-eared notebook she used to take notes during the lessons. She'd figured out pretty early that you couldn't be a dance mom without a little steno pad full of choreography, and she had to admit it was helpful whenever Ellie wanted to practice at home and Jessie was at a loss for the proper name for 'that move where your back leg is straight out behind you' or something like that. She didn't have a mind for memorizing the ballet terms, but Ellie sure did.

"Arabesque," she'd chided Jessie as she swept her back foot into the position. "It's one of the first ones I learned."

After that, Jessie started carrying around the notebook.

"Got it," she muttered, snatching it up from beneath her grocery store vest on the back seat.

Jessie followed Ellie into the lobby, where they found Melody already warming up in the studio. She was wearing the same pink sweater she wore when she taught the beginner class despite the warmth of the studio, and Jessie watched for a moment as she moved through a series of fluid leg movements at the barre.

Then Ellie burst into the room, yelling excitedly for Melody and disrupting her flow.

"Hi, Ellie," Melody said cheerfully, bending down to accept Ellie's customary hug and then glancing over at Jessie as she straightened up. "Good morning."

"Good morning," Jessie said, trying to make her voice as business-like as possible. "I'm just going to sit out of the way over here and take notes for Ellie, if that's okay."

"Help yourself," Melody said with a smile that felt a little bit more than friendly.

It made something stir in Jessie's core, and she bit her

lip self-consciously as she slid into one of the chairs lining the wall where the moms usually sat. She watched Melody walk over to the stereo on the wall, her pace graceful and deliberate. Jessie couldn't tear her eyes off her, and neither could Ellie, although for very different reasons. Ellie was pacing back and forth across the floor, trying to mimic the ballet walk that Melody had just done, watching her carefully in case she did it again on her way back to the center of the room.

When Melody turned and saw her doing it, she smiled and said, "It's a little more like this. Sweep your back foot behind you, toes down to the floor, as you step forward."

Ellie and Jessie both watched entranced as Melody walked across the room, practically floating, and Jessie's breath caught in her throat as she realized that Melody was making a line straight for her. She'd stop soon – she'd have to stop soon – but as the classical music built to a crescendo on the stereo, Melody just kept pacing closer and closer to Jessie.

The closer she came, the more the rest of the room faded away. Jessie even lost sight of Ellie for a moment as everything ceased to exist except Melody. She stopped no more than six inches from Jessie's chair, looking down and giving her a smoldering look. Jessie suddenly felt hot all over, especially in her neck and cheeks, and she thought if she reached out and touched Melody, she would be able to see the static arcing between their bodies.

Then Melody smiled and turned, waltzing back to

the center of the room and beginning the lesson. "It's just like that. You try now, Ellie."

Jessie had to struggle not to visibly slump in her chair, and she was breathing a little heavier than necessary. That moment brought her immediately back to the recital and the way their bodies had come together just before they were interrupted. Her heart ached for Melody. These private lessons would be the death of her, because no matter how many romance novels she read, none of them could hold a candle to her.

She'd known the contents of her heart since she was sixteen, and yet no one had ever made her mourn that part of her life before. It had been off-limits ever since she married Steve and Ellie was born. The longer she sat there and stared at Melody, completely absorbed in teaching Ellie how to perform an *assemble,* the more Jessie was certain that there was something major missing in her life, and that Melody could give it to her if only the fates allowed it.

THE MOMENT JESSIE FEARED – being alone with Melody – came right after the lesson ended. Jessie handed Ellie a change of clothes and told her to go into the bathroom and get dressed for school. Ellie dashed out, and then Jessie and Melody were alone in the studio.

It would have been so much better if they had enough time to go home after the lesson and change there – it would eliminate this awkward moment of waiting with Melody. Jessie thought about helping Ellie with her clothes, but she was old enough to dress herself and also old enough to get irritable when she sensed Jessie was breathing down her neck too much. She should stay out here with Melody if for no other reason than to nurture her daughter's independence.

So Jessie looked down at her notepad and saw that she hadn't written down a single thing in the last hour. She'd missed every single ballet term Melody threw out because she'd been totally absorbed in watching the way Melody moved so gracefully and fluidly across the floor.

Melody came over to where Jessie was sitting and said, "What did you think?"

"Huh?"

"Was I worth the money or are you going to ask Mary Beth for a refund?" Melody asked with a smirk that attempted to disguise genuine self-doubt.

"No," Jessie said, surprised. "You were fantastic. So good, in fact, that I forgot to take notes. What was that last thing you taught her? The jumping one?"

"Changement," Melody said, never taking her wide chestnut eyes off Jessie as she demonstrated the move again for her.

Jessie jotted it down – truth be told, she didn't give a damn about changements or any of the other moves right now. Suddenly, all she really wanted to do was shove Melody up against the nearest wall and find out if the kiss she'd been fantasizing about would feel as good as she always thought it would. She stood up and Melody didn't step back. There were less than twelve inches separating them.

Jessie could feel the heat from Melody's body. Her eyes lingered on Melody's lips. She couldn't quite convince herself to go for it, and instead she asked tentatively, "Umm, same time next week?"

"Yeah," Melody said, and Jessie couldn't be sure – the motion was so subtle – but she thought Melody was leaning in toward her again, just like she had at the recital last year.

"Okay," Jessie said, dodging away from Melody in a blind panic and knocking her knees into the folding chairs against the wall in the process. It made a horrible racket as metal collided with metal.

She was halfway across the studio floor before Melody called, "Is that all?"

Jessie turned around. "What do you mean?"

"You know what I mean."

Jessie took a few steps toward Melody, then caught herself and stopped. She looked at her from a safe distance of about five feet and shrugged, saying quietly, "I have to think about my husband."

"Why?" Melody asked, a hint of incredulity rising into her voice, but when Jessie shot her a shocked look, the mirth died down. Instead, she looked mildly annoyed.

Melody put her hands on her hips, looking about as frustrated as Jessie felt, and the sleeves of her sweater inched up her arms. Jessie saw something pink on Melody's forearm – a large scar – and her mouth dropped open slightly. Melody noticed the direction of Jessie's eyes, and her cheeks and neck went immediately pink as she looked away, shoving her sleeves back down.

"What's that?" Jessie asked carefully.

Melody wouldn't look at her. All the mirrors in the room made it easy to see her face, though, and it was clear that she was suddenly trying not to cry. "Nothing."

"I'm sorry," Jessie offered, worried that she had upset Melody. "I should go."

She started to turn away again – Ellie would be tearing up the hall any minute, or else she was trapped in her leotard and in need of help. Either way, Jessie needed to get out of this studio. But then she heard Melody's voice, low as she asked, "Does he know you're gay?"

Jessie paused in the door, one hand on the frame, and after a second she said quietly, "No."

Then she met Ellie coming into the lobby – *great timing, kid, thanks* – and they walked out of the school.

CHAPTER NINETEEN

JESSIE

I think I'm in trouble.

That was the content of the note Jessie passed to her best friend, Blaire, in history class the day she finally got up the courage to work out the math on her calendar. It had been two months since she agreed to go on a double-date with Blaire and her boyfriend and his buddy Steve, and three months since her last period.

Blaire passed a note back as soon as their teacher looked away, saying something snarky about how forgetting to study for a test is only a state of emergency in Jessie's world. Jessie scribbled a plea to meet outside of the building after school – she couldn't bring herself to write exactly what she was dreading on a piece of paper.

"What's the big crisis?" Blaire asked as soon as she found Jessie at the end of the day.

"I need you to go to the drug store with me," Jessie said, her cheeks already turning red. She didn't want to say what she was about to say, but there was no getting around it. She leaned in and whispered close to Blaire's ear, "I think I'm pregnant."

"What?!" Blaire shrieked, and Jessie winced and almost had to cover her ears.

"Shh!" She hissed, and people turned their heads as they walked past the two of them.

"From who?" Blaire whispered. "Not Steve. Not on your first time."

Jessie could do nothing but shrug pathetically, and Blaire gave her a sympathetic look that bordered on abject horror, putting her arm around Jessie's shoulder. Jessie leaned into it, picking up the coconut scent of Blaire's hair as she led them down the steps of the school.

"Well, let's not get too worried until we're sure," Blaire said, trying to sound comforting, but Jessie was plenty worried.

She didn't even know Steve – not really. She'd only agreed to go on that stupid double date because Blaire wanted another couple to hang out with and it seemed to Jessie like an acceptable sacrifice to make in order to spend more time with her best friend. Blaire had turned into a ghost the moment she started dating Josh, and all Jessie wanted was her friend back. Steve turned out to be a nice guy, but they hadn't so much as looked at each other in the halls ever since their date and the thought of telling him she was carrying his child made Jessie sick to her stomach. Or maybe those were the pregnancy hormones.

They climbed into Jessie's Sebring, little specks of rust flaking off from the edges of the doors, and they drove to the drug store down the street from her house. Blaire took one for the team when Jessie blanched at the idea of going up to the counter and plunking down a pregnancy test, and then they went back to Jessie's house. Mercifully it was empty, and they both scurried upstairs to the bathroom.

Blaire tore open the box and handed Jessie a plastic stick, then pulled out a sheet of instructions.

"Well?" Jessie asked.

"I think you know what you have to do," Blaire said sympathetically. "After that, we wait five minutes. If you're... you know... it'll have two blue lines."

"Okay," Jessie said with a huge, shaky sigh. "Turn around."

Blaire faced the bathtub while Jessie peed on the stick, and then she laid it on a tissue on the counter beside her.

"Now we wait," she said, lowering the toilet lid and sitting down anxiously. Her heart was slamming against her chest and she didn't think she could wait the five minutes to find out her fate.

Blaire sat on the edge of the bathtub across from her and when she saw how nervous Jessie was, she took her hand. Jessie looked down at their intertwined fingers – something she never would have dared to do if Blaire hadn't reached for her first. Jessie felt that touch all the way up her arms – it tingled, warm and pleasant in a way that holding a boy's hand had never done for her. Steve certainly didn't have this kind of effect on her – she wouldn't have slept with him at all if Blaire and Josh hadn't gone, pawing at each other, into her room at the end of the night and left Steve looking expectantly at her.

At the time she thought it was what a sixteen-year-old girl was supposed to do, and supposed to want to do.

"Jess," Blaire said softly. "Look at me."

Her eyes traced up from Blaire's hands to her eyes, light blue like the sky, and suddenly Jessie was sure that the way she felt whenever she looked into Blaire's eyes was the way most girls felt about boys. It may have taken her ten years of friendship to come to that conclusion, but as they sat in her bathroom, waiting for a little plastic stick to decide her fate, Jessie realized that she was in love with her best friend.

"We're going to get through this, no matter what it says," Blaire said, nodding to the stick.

For an instant, Jessie wondered what would happen if she leaned over and kissed her. And then Blaire picked up the stick, pinching it between the tissue and turning it away from Jessie.

"Are you ready?"

"No," Jessie said, squeezing Blaire's hand even tighter and keeping her eyes locked on Blaire's. If she got so lost in those sky blue eyes, maybe she could fall into them, pause this moment, and never hear the next words out of Blaire's mouth.

No such luck, though. Jessie was beginning to realize just how unlucky she was.

Blaire took a deep breath, squeezed Jessie's hand, and looked at the stick. "Two lines."

Jessie let out a huge exhalation. She didn't even realize she'd been holding her breath, and suddenly it felt like all the air had gone out of the room.

There you have it, *she thought. In the space of five minutes, she figured out why every romantic interaction she'd ever had with a boy felt wrong and she also realized that none of it mattered anymore. She would have to tell Steve about the baby, they would almost definitely get married because that was what pregnant teenagers in Lisbon did, and that would be the end of it.*

CHAPTER TWENTY

MELODY

Melody wasn't quite sure how her next interaction with Jessie would go after she couldn't resist asking about her husband, and more importantly after Jessie saw the jagged pink scar on her forearm. She would have given anything to keep it from her – she would have accosted Jessie about the state of her marriage a hundred times if she could have just kept her sleeve from riding up and revealing that.

There were only four people in the whole world who had seen her scar, if she didn't count the emergency room doctors in New York and the one in Lisbon who removed the stitches about a week after she came home. Her mother and father had seen it while they were changing her bandages in the hospital. Dr. Riley saw it because she insisted that it had been intentional and Melody thought showing her the jagged nature of it would convince her to believe she had the flu and had collapsed down the wall (whole lot of good that did).

And Starla saw it, not because Melody wanted her to but because she was a nosy little kid who thought the world revolved around her and she needed to know exactly how fucked up her big sister was. She hid in the bathroom one day when Melody was getting ready to shower, peeking around the curtain until she pulled her long-sleeve tee shirt over her head and then popping out to ogle the scar and scare the hell out of Melody in the process.

Melody had caught every single one of them glancing surreptitiously at her arm after they'd seen the scar, and she knew when they looked at her now, they didn't see Melody the ballerina, or even Melody the *failed* ballerina. They saw Melody the suicide attempt because not one of them believed her when she said it was an accident. Of course they wouldn't – not with everything going against her when it happened.

And now Jessie had seen it – not all of its six-inch, keloid-laden glory, but enough.

Melody didn't even make eye contact with her when she brought Ellie for the Saturday afternoon beginner's class, finding a reason to turn around at the desk and hide her face until they'd both disappeared into the studio. It was a bit harder to avoid Jessie when it was time for Ellie's second private lesson, though, and for that Melody wore a thick warm-up hoodie with thumb holes in the cuffs of the sleeves. She used to wear it jogging and she'd probably sweat like hell in it, but at least there was no risk of her sleeve creeping up again.

"Good morning," she said to Ellie as she came into

the studio, summoning every bit of cheer she could muster so Ellie wouldn't sense the tension between her mother and Melody. "Are you ready to learn the rond de jambe?"

"Are you teaching my daughter nonsense words now?" Jessie asked with a smile as she followed her daughter into the room, and Melody was surprised to find her in a joking mood. No one ever joked with her after they saw the scar – they all assumed she was too fragile for that kind of thing.

"That's right," she shot back, "and later we'll learn the futterwacken."

"Excuse me?" Jessie asked with a raised eyebrow.

Melody laughed. "Futterwacken. It's the Mad Hatter's dance in *Alice in Wonderland*."

"Sounds fun," Ellie said. "I want to do it!"

"Okay," Melody said with another little laugh. "Rond de jambe first, though."

Ellie went into the middle of the room and sat down on the floor, ready to run through all of the usual warm-up exercises. The kid was a sponge and there were very few moves that Melody had to teach her more than once – it reminded Melody a lot of her own early ballet lessons.

Ballet was like breathing to her in a lot of ways, natural and effortless. At least, that's how it felt when she was doing it for fun, and when she was the star ballerina in a small town with not much competition. When she got to New York and had to square off against the cream of the crop, she realized pretty quickly that she still had a lot to learn and it wasn't nearly so fun or effortless.

Melody taught Ellie a few new moves – futterwacken not included on account of the fact that Melody couldn't actually remember what it looked like – and Jessie sat in the corner quietly taking notes the whole time, rarely glancing at Melody.

After the lesson ended and Jessie and Ellie dashed out of the studio to drop Ellie off at school, Melody found herself alone in the studio. The next class wasn't until the afternoon, and she noted with surprise that she didn't feel the need to immediately peel off her leotard like a parasite clinging to her. Instead, she lingered in the studio for a little while.

She retrieved her phone and watched a couple videos of the futterwacken scene from *Alice in Wonderland*, walking her way through a few tentative steps as she did so. It was really more of a liquid dancing style, but Melody figured out a few moves she could modify into a short ballet routine. She set her phone down and walked into the center of the room, watching herself in the large, wall-to-wall mirror as she tested them out.

She ran through the routine a couple of times after she decided on the choreography, committing it to memory so she could teach it to Ellie next week, and then she picked up her phone and went into the bathroom to change. It was the first time she'd danced voluntarily since she came home, and she wasn't quite sure how she felt about it yet.

As she changed into a pair of jeans and a sweater for

her shift at the reception desk later in the day, Melody thought again about how much Ellie reminded her of a young version of herself. She remembered those early-morning private lessons well, and that was when the ballet bug bit her. It was hard not to feel special, destined for something greater than an end-of-year recital, when the whole world was asleep but you and your teacher were up before dawn working toward something.

Melody wasn't quite sure how she felt about that yet, either. Sometimes it felt noble to pass down her ballet knowledge to a newcomer, and other times when she thought about it, she couldn't get over the fear that she was pushing Ellie toward the path that she'd gone down without warning her of the dangers ahead. For Melody, it started out with a private lesson once a week, and then it was twice a week, and then every day, and then before she knew it her whole world was dance and she didn't know anything else.

It didn't seem fair to do that to someone else.

DOCTOR RILEY SEEMED QUITE interested in the developments at work. Melody avoided telling her about being forced to cover the beginner ballet class a few weeks ago out of fear that she'd see it as a step forward. It had been coercion, plain and simple, regardless of how much Melody ended up enjoying it.

She didn't even tell her about the private lessons right away, despite the fact that keeping them a secret made

Melody feel guilty. Her parents didn't have an unlimited supply of money to spend on therapy sessions in which she withheld pertinent information. But she was afraid that Dr. Riley would see those private lessons as too much of a breakthrough, and Melody felt just as fucked up as ever.

She couldn't keep it all bottled up forever though, and the nagging fear that she was contributing to Ellie's journey down the same path she'd gone down herself was what finally caused Melody to cave. She told Dr. Riley about the private lessons, and then spent a good twenty minutes of her session expounding on her concerns about Ellie.

"I just can't stop worrying that I'm contributing to someone else's future mental breakdown," Melody said, throwing up her hands when she'd said all she could on the matter.

Dr. Riley had listened silently and attentively during Melody's long rant, and when she finished, Dr. Riley set her notepad down in her lap and said, "Ellie isn't you."

It was a bit curt, and it rankled a little.

"She might not end up being as interested in ballet as you are," Dr. Riley said, to which Melody broke in with a past-tense correction of *were*. Dr. Riley modified her statement and went on. "Okay, *were*. Maybe for Ellie, it doesn't go beyond the level of hobby, or maybe it does and she has a different set of coping tools than you had available to you. I'll say it again. Ellie isn't you."

"I know that."

"Do you?" Dr. Riley challenged. "I think you're

projecting a lot of your own insecurities onto Ellie. How do you feel about the fact that you're giving private lessons to the daughter of this woman you feel attracted to?"

"What does that have to do with anything?" Melody asked.

"I just think it might complicate your feelings about being in the studio," Dr. Riley said with a shrug. She was trying very hard to be casual, but Melody could tell she was driving at something. After a moment's pause, during which she was sure Dr. Riley was hoping Melody would jump in and supply her own theory, Dr. Riley asked, "Do you think it's possible that you're disguising the apprehension you feel about Jessie as a concern for Ellie's well-being? Maybe if you focus your energy on Ellie, you won't have to think about the possibility of truly opening up to Jessie, or even the fact that you've already begun to face your fears by going into the studio in the first place."

"I'm not afraid to open up," Melody said defensively.

"But you panicked when she saw your scar," Dr. Riley pointed out. "It sounds like you're still hiding parts of yourself from her."

"What difference would it make if I did open up? She's married."

"Yes," Dr. Riley said. "She's married, and you have talked about her in every one of our sessions since you met her. Whether it's viable to try to be with her or not, your heart is making its desires known."

"That's not fair," Melody said. "You're the one who brought her up this time."

"It sounds like she has a calming effect on you," Dr. Riley said, ignoring Melody's accusation.

Melody thought about last year's dance recital and the panic attack she'd had watching from the wings of the stage. She'd gone outside to get fresh air and slow the racing of her pulse, and when Jessie appeared it was like the whole world slowed down. And then there was the day when she had to cover the beginner ballet class for Mary Beth, and Jessie had brought her racing pulse back down with nothing more than a smile and a few words.

"So what?"

"Sounds like talking to Jessie is a much better way of coping with the stresses of the world than smoking weed," Dr. Riley said. "Maybe what you're really worried about isn't the possibility of Ellie traveling down the same path as you. Maybe you're worried that the more time you spend in the studio with her, the closer you'll get to her mother, and getting closer to Jessie just might force you to give up the belief you've picked up since you came home that life ends after Pavlova. Does that sound fair?"

"I guess so," Melody said reluctantly.

"Good," Dr. Riley said, jotting something quickly on her legal pad. She smiled at Melody as she looked up again and said, "I'd call that progress. Since there's not a lot you can do about Jessie's marital status, I think it would be constructive to approach this fear of yours from a different angle. Do you think having a stronger support system would have given you the tools you needed to handle the pressure better when you were in New York?"

"Maybe."

"I want to give you a homework assignment, then," Dr. Riley said, sitting forward in her chair. Melody could tell she was excited about whatever she was about to present. "I want you to think about the kind of teacher and mentor you would have wanted when you were younger, and then work on being that for Ellie."

Melody thought about this for a minute or two, then smiled. "Yeah, okay. I like that. It's kind of like watching my younger self get a do-over and preventing New York from happening again."

"Exactly," Dr. Riley said, then looked down at her watch. "Well, that's the end of our session. I think we got a lot accomplished today. You should be proud."

CHAPTER TWENTY-ONE

JESSIE

A fter a few weeks of private lessons, Jessie started to notice a bond forming between Melody and Ellie. Melody would chat with her while they were putting their ballet slippers on, asking her about school and the other things she liked to do besides ballet, and she even took the time to create a practice schedule for Ellie to use when she wasn't in the studio.

"Come here," Melody said to Ellie one day at the end of class, then she approached Jessie sitting along the wall of the studio.

Jessie tried not to look up from her notepad – she wasn't all that eager to make eye contact with Melody because ever since she'd started reading those damn romance novels she couldn't stop filling in Melody's face for all the heroines. It felt wrong to look at her after all the intimate moments they'd shared in her imagination. But the closer Melody came, the more curious Jessie got, and she looked up.

Melody waltzed her way gracefully across the floor, Ellie following behind like a miniature version of her, and they both stopped right in front of Jessie. Ellie thought this was great fun, giggling and waiting to see what Melody had up her sleeve, and for just a moment time froze as Melody and Jessie locked eyes.

Then she leaned over and put her hand on Jessie's notepad. "Can I borrow this?"

"Umm," Jessie stuttered. "Yeah."

She let Melody slide the pad out of her fingers, then handed over the pen as well. Melody sat down cross-legged in front of her and Ellie plopped down beside Melody.

"How much time do you think you spend each week doing ballet?" Melody asked Ellie.

"I don't know," Ellie said, glancing at Jessie for help.

"A *lot*," Jessie said with a laugh. "I'm not sure you've crossed a room without chasséing since you started taking classes."

"Nice, you remembered a ballet term," Melody said, grinning at Jessie and holding her hand out for a high five. For a second she wasn't sure Jessie would play along, but then she reached out and gave Melody's palm a quick slap.

"It would be impossible to spend this much time in a dance studio and not pick up anything at all," Jessie answered. "I'd say between lessons and the endless practicing at home, Ellie spends upwards of ten hours a week in her ballet slippers."

"Hmm, that's no good," Melody said with a frown, tapping the pen against her lips as she thought.

It was an innocent gesture, but it made Jessie's imagination go wild and she couldn't tear her eyes off the pen as it bounced against Melody's plump lower lip. She wasn't here for that – she was here for Ellie to learn ballet, and that was all. She thought off-hand that it might be best if she started dropping Ellie off and running errands during this class too, or just sitting in her car until the private lesson was over. Ellie was old enough now to be alone for a little while, and she was clearly comfortable with Melody.

"It's not?" Ellie asked, looking dismayed.

"Well, you have to give your muscles a chance to rest and it's also not good to forget about stuff like your friends just because you'd rather do ballet," Melody said. Ellie nodded like she understood but wasn't quite sure she liked what she was hearing. "Here's what we're going to do to make sure you're the best ballerina you can be without wearing yourself out. We're going to create a ballet schedule for you, okay?"

Ellie watched as Melody drew a few lines on the notepad, dividing it into seven days. They spent the next few minutes blocking out Ellie's week into school, homework, chores, sleep, ballet, and down time. Melody gave her half an hour every weekday evening for optional ballet practice, plus her two lessons a week.

"There you go," Melody said. "That's four and a half hours of ballet each week, and at that rate you'll be a prima ballerina in no time flat. Outside of that time, though, I don't want you in those ballet slippers for anything, got it?"

"Okay," Ellie said reluctantly.

"Maybe next year we'll revisit that, but in the mean time you're a kid – go outside and play," Melody said with a laugh.

"And right now you better go get changed," Jessie said, checking her watch and seeing that it was almost time to drop Ellie off at school. "Go on, hurry up, bug."

Ellie got up from the floor and dashed out of the studio, and Melody handed the notebook back to Jessie.

"I hope that schedule works for you," she said. "You can always adjust it, of course. I just thought she might be wearing herself a little thin with the ballet."

"Thanks," Jessie said, taking the notebook back a little too quickly as she jerked it out of Melody's hand.

It was unintentional, but Melody noticed the edge in her voice. There had been an awful lot of *we* in that conversation – *we will revisit that.* Jessie hadn't signed up for all this one-on-one time with Melody when she agreed to private lessons for Ellie, and she wasn't sure if she could handle another year or two of the tension that rose between them whenever they were alone in a room together.

"Something wrong?" Melody asked as she stood up from the floor. Jessie stood too, eager to get out of such close quarters with her. The temptation was too great, and she'd feel better in the lobby.

"You know you're just supposed to be teaching her enough so she can move up to the intermediate class with her friends next year, right?" Jessie snapped. "She's not trying out for Pavlova."

The look on Melody's face stopped Jessie dead in her tracks. It was like she'd slapped her across the cheek.

"What?" Jessie asked, surprised.

"Who told you?" Melody's voice went cold and it was so unlike her.

"Told me what?" Jessie asked.

"About my history," she said. "Did Mary Beth tell you about Pavlova to convince you to let me teach Ellie?"

"I don't know what you're talking about," Jessie said, dumbfounded. "She recommended you highly."

"Never mind," Melody said, heading out of the studio and going to her customary place behind the reception desk.

Jessie followed her out to the lobby, and Ellie was still in the restroom getting changed for school. She checked her watch again, feeling a little restless because these mornings were always a hectic dash to get Ellie to school on time and then make it across town for her grocery store shift. But she couldn't ignore the way that Melody was pointedly looking away from her. She'd clearly struck a nerve, and Jessie didn't feel right leaving the subject on such a terse note.

"I'm sorry. I didn't mean to upset you," she said, leaning against the reception desk ledge and making sure to keep her voice soft.

As hard as it was to spend so much time with Melody, it was harder to keep her passions under control around her. Jessie had spent the last six years of her life trying to be numb because it seemed better to feel nothing than to mourn a life she could never have, but Melody had shattered that well-protected numbness. Jessie could never go back to not caring about her.

When Melody's eyes flitted up to Jessie's and then back down to the desk, busying herself with the ledger, Jessie added quietly, "I didn't mean anything by that comment about Pavlova. Did you go there?"

Melody repeated the subconscious gesture Jessie had seen a few times before and thought nothing of, rubbing her wrist down over her thigh so as to tug her sweater sleeve down. This time, though, she thought of the glimpse of a scar she'd seen on Melody's wrist the other day. Melody had gotten so bent out of shape about it, she didn't want to push her on the matter.

"Yes," Melody said, still not meeting Jessie's eyes. "I dropped out after my first semester. Or left in shame, to be more accurate."

She glanced up at Jessie, catching her looking at her wrist, and a heavy silence settled between them. Then Melody sighed and unlooped her thumb from the hole of her sweater, yanking it up to her elbow and revealing a large pink scar. Jessie gasped, then immediately felt guilty for such a knee-jerk reaction.

Melody didn't give her a chance to ask questions. She said, "I was delirious with the worst stomach flu of my life right before a huge audition and I slipped and cut myself in the shower. No one believes it was an accident – not even my parents – because I'd been falling farther and farther behind the rest of the dancers in my class. They all thought I did it to get out of the audition, or out of the school, and the truth was that I was relieved when I realized it was an excuse to come home. I had to lose two pints of blood to get out of there, and I'm still paying for it every day with guilt and a newfound sense of uselessness."

She pulled down her sleeve, looping her thumb back into the hole to keep the fabric over her wrist.

"You're not useless," Jessie tried to object, but Melody continued as if she was afraid to stop lest she lose her nerve.

"I've never told anyone that except for my therapist," she said. "Not even my parents. So please keep it to yourself. The reason I'm telling you is as a cautionary tale. I was just like Ellie at her age – a precocious kid with a singular interest in ballet. I started dancing around the same age, and I took private lessons at a studio similar to this one. Just keep an eye on her and make sure she doesn't end up tying her identity into her ballet slippers like I did."

Jessie just stared at Melody, at a loss for words, and that's when Ellie finally came down the hall in her school clothes, ballet bag slung over her shoulder.

"Have a good week, Ellie," Melody said, turning on the charm again and shaking loose the darkness that had settled between them. Then she turned to Jessie and said somberly, "Bye, Jess."

"Bye," Jessie said, taking Ellie by the hand and leading her out the door. They would most definitely be late to school and work today.

RECITAL SEASON SNUCK up on Jessie. It hardly felt like an entire year had passed since Ellie began attending Mary Beth's School of Dance, and yet there she was prancing through the living room in a sparkly tutu all her own.

"Turn around and put your arms up," Jessie instructed, putting a couple of pins between her lips as Ellie came over to her.

She had two costumes – a navy, sequined tutu for her beginner ballet class's routine, and a pretty blush-pink and flowing skirt that matched her ballet slippers for her private lessons with Melody. The tutu, unfortunately, required a bit of sewing to attach the spaghetti straps at the top of the leotard, so Jessie had Ellie put it on and she reluctantly got out the needle and thread. One thing was for sure – if Ellie stuck with ballet, Jessie's seamstress skills were sure to improve.

Ellie hadn't wanted to take the tutu off after Jessie finished pinning the straps in place, and it had been equally hard to keep her out of the costumes for the week and a half between when Jessie picked them up and the day of the recital. They got there eventually though, even if it did feel like the longest week of Jessie's life.

This year, they went to the high school on recital night as a family, Ellie chattering excitedly to Steve as he drove and Jessie held onto the mounds of tulle and silk that made up Ellie's costumes.

"I want you to meet my teachers and all my friends,"

she was saying as they pulled into the lot. "Mommy already knows everybody but you don't know any of them."

"I'm just looking forward to seeing you dance on that big stage," Steve said, smiling at Ellie through the rear view mirror. "Are you excited?"

"Don't egg her on, she might shoot through the roof," Jessie teased.

They went into the building, where a few dozen students in different types of costumes were milling around in the hall, figuring out where they needed to go and greeting their relatives as the auditorium filled.

"Come on, daddy!" Ellie cried, taking Steve and Jessie each by the hand and dragging them down the hall in search of her classmates. They were halfway down the hall, Ellie's two costumes draped over Jessie's arm, when she saw Melody coming toward them. Jessie noticed her glancing at Steve, no doubt guessing who he was, and then Melody was smiling and bending down to give Ellie her customary hug.

"Are you ready for the stage?" She asked with a big grin.

"Yep, I got my costumes right there," Ellie said. "This is my daddy. You haven't met him yet."

"No, I haven't," Melody said, standing up and extending her hand to Steve. "Melody Bledsoe. I'm one of Ellie's teachers."

"Steve Cartwright," he answered, shaking her hand. "You teach the beginner class?"

"No, I teach Ellie's private lessons," she said, her eyes

darting to Jessie and then back to Steve in a look that Jessie hoped he didn't catch. Jessie felt color rising into her cheeks.

"Oh," he said, with an odd, tentative inflection. Jessie couldn't be sure, but she thought she saw him raise his eyebrows momentarily. It had to be imagined, a product of guilt for all those shifts spent inserting Melody's name into her romance novels. Jessie's heart beat a little faster nevertheless.

"You should be really proud of your daughter," Melody went on, not noticing the strained expression on Steve's face. She didn't know him like Jessie did. "Getting a solo dance in your first year is a pretty big deal."

"Well, I better help Ellie get into her first costume," Jessie said. She couldn't stand in the hallway between her husband and her fantasy girl any longer, and Ellie was having trouble standing still anyway. She was tugging impatiently on Jessie's hand. "Steve, I have to help Ellie get dressed. The auditorium is through that door. Save me a seat toward the front?"

"Sure, Jess," he said, and his voice seemed a little more curt than she was used to.

CHAPTER TWENTY-TWO

STEVE

Steve found a couple of seats toward the front of the auditorium, throwing his coat over the back of one of them to reserve it for Jessie. She might have trouble finding him if the house lights went off before she managed to get Ellie into her costume, but for the moment he didn't much care.

He saw the way Ellie's teacher looked at Jessie before she noticed Steve standing beside her. He knew that look, even if it hadn't been directed at him in a long time. There was chemistry between them and it made his stomach hurt.

Ever since he found that lesbian book on Jessie's phone, Steve wasn't sure what to do with that information. He couldn't just ask her over breakfast one day if she was still playing for his team, and it seemed like bringing it up at all might be an over-reaction. People read books about Jeffrey Dahmer and they weren't serial killers, and they watched Game of Thrones even if they

179

weren't attracted to their siblings. Maybe it was just a good book with a plot that caught Jessie's eye. He had pretty much decided to let it go, but then he saw Jessie blush when she looked at Ellie's teacher. Now he couldn't get that damn book out of his head again.

When Jessie found him, the lights were going down and he snatched his coat off the back of her chair then crossed his arms in front of his chest. He'd had just enough time sitting alone in the auditorium to get good and indignant as she sat down beside him. Five years of marriage - five years of thinking his wife was frigid or maybe he was just plain repulsive, and now he had to wonder if she just hadn't bothered to tell him his cock was the problem.

"Ellie's first dance is the group one," Jessie leaned over to whisper to him. "It's about fifteen minutes into the recital."

"Mmpfhh," Steve grunted, acknowledging that he'd heard her and making it clear he had no interest in talking. It was petty but he didn't care right now. Was she fooling around with that instructor? Was that what they were doing every Tuesday morning at the crack of dawn, laughing at his cluelessness while he slept alone?

Ellie's first dance was the fourth one in the show, but in Steve's current mood it felt like two hours instead of fifteen minutes before she went on. He softened up a bit when he saw Ellie walk onto the stage, beaming the entire time and performing every move with precision and a natural grace. He'd seen the dance a thousand times already in his living room, but he watched every step with pride swelling in his chest. For those three minutes he forgot about Jessie sitting beside him and the feeling of betrayal building inside him.

Steve clapped loudly as the beginner ballet class scurried off the stage, standing up so that Ellie could spot him beyond the stage lights and read the pride in his face. Then when Ellie was gone and Steve sank back into his chair, Jessie leaned over to him again. It was all he could do not to recoil from her.

"I'm going to meet her in the hallway," she whispered as the next group of kids, tap dancers, came onto the stage. "I have to help her get into the next costume."

"Fine," Steve said curtly.

Jessie got up and made her way as quietly as she could out of the auditorium, and Steve was left with his thoughts again, watching a bunch of kids he didn't know perform dance routines he didn't care about, while for all he knew, his wife was off having a quick tryst with a gorgeous, young ballet teacher. That was just great.

CHAPTER TWENTY-THREE

JESSIE

J essie went down the hall toward the stage door. Ellie didn't stand a chance of getting out of that tight tutu by herself – she was growing like a weed lately and the thing was a bear to get on her in the first place – and there were only three numbers separating her first and second routines so they'd have to work fast.

Ellie wasn't in the hall when Jessie got to the stage door, but Melody was. They literally smacked into each other as Jessie approached and Melody opened the door from within, rushing out to get the next group of dancers.

"Oh," Jessie gasped as their bodies collided, her hands going out to steady herself and finding Melody's hips on accident. Her head filled with Melody's peppermint scent and suddenly she was feeling a little dizzy.

"Whoa," Melody said, her lips close to Jessie's ear, and she could feel the vibration of Melody's voice. It sent a shiver through her whole body and she was acutely aware of the way her hands were lingering on Melody's hips.

"I'm sorry," she said, but she didn't let go. She couldn't let go.

"My fault," Melody said, those gorgeous round eyes coming up to meet Jessie's gaze.

They hadn't been this close since last year's recital, in the moment when they almost kissed. Jessie spent an entire year thinking about that moment and expanding it into a whole series of fantasies in which she got the girl and Melody's lips tasted exactly as good as they looked.

She could do it now. It wouldn't be anything to lean in a few more inches and press her lips against Melody's. The way those chestnut eyes were studying her, Jessie knew Melody was waiting for her to do just that.

"What the hell is going on here?"

The words were not spoken in anger, but they made Jessie's blood run cold nonetheless. Everything slowed down and it was like watching a reaction sequence play out in slow motion. Steve's voice echoed down the hall and Jessie watched Melody's eyes go wide with surprise as she looked over Jessie's shoulder.

Then Jessie jerked her hands away from Melody's hips, spinning around to face her husband. He was standing ten feet away from them with a look of betrayal on his face.

"I have to go," Melody said quietly. "I have to get the next group."

Then she hurried down the hall toward the dressing

room and Jessie didn't blame her for running away from this mess. She told herself that given the opportunity, she would not have actually kissed Melody. Hadn't they had a few dozen opportunities in the last year? She resisted them all, but Steve hadn't seen that just like he hadn't seen the way they collided in the hall. It just looked bad out of context.

"Steve-" Jessie began, her heart racing with guilt while shame burned in her cheeks.

His lips were pressed together, his face red, and if she wasn't mistaken, there were tears threatening the corners of his eyes. It was a little disconcerting – after five years of utilitarian marriage, Jessie had no idea he was even capable of having such strong emotions about her.

"Are you with her?" he asked quietly.

They had the hall to themselves for now, but it wouldn't last – not with Melody and Mary Beth running around corralling kids – and Ellie was probably waiting for Jessie in the dressing room, eager to change out of the tutu and put on her next costume.

"No," Jessie said. "No, of course not."

"Don't lie to me, Jess," Steve said, his voice taking on a pleading tone that made Jessie want to cry. "I know."

"Know what?"

How could he know the contents of her heart, the fantasies she tried to content herself with, or even the quiet glances she and Melody shared over the reception desk? Jessie spent most of the last year confused and tormented, so how could he possibly know what it all meant when she didn't?

"I know about the books you've been reading," he said, his tone taking on a slightly more petulant quality. "I saw them. I *read* them."

"Books?"

"The lesbian books," Steve hissed, trying not to raise his voice so it wouldn't travel down the hall.

That word shot through Jessie like a lightning bolt, frying her nerves as she realized he must have looked in her phone at some point and found the ebooks she'd used to spark her fantasies about Melody. Another wave of guilt washed over her and suddenly Steve's moodiness in the auditorium made sense. He *had* noticed that look Melody gave her after all and he was upset about it, coupled with Jessie's choice of reading material.

How long ago did he find those books, though? Now that Jessie thought about it, he'd been distant for a while. In the rare moments when they spent more than five minutes together, he only wanted to talk about their work schedules and Ellie's homework and who was going to do the grocery shopping that week. He never seemed to want to be in the same room as Jessie anymore, and she just hadn't noticed because she was too busy juggling everything else. That had begun months ago – how long had he been holding all of this in? Probably not longer than Jessie had been bottling up her feelings for Melody.

"You're not the person I thought you were," he said. "How could you lie to me for so long?"

"Steve-" Jessie tried again, but he didn't let her finish. That was okay because even if he let her speak, she had no idea what the rest of that sentence would have been.

There was nothing to say and no comfort to give in this situation and all Jessie could do was look at the disappointment in Steve's eyes.

He took his keyring out of the pocket of his jeans and plopped it into Jessie's hand.

"Take the car," he said. "Tell Ellie I'm really sorry I missed her solo. I can't be in the same building as you and that ballet instructor right now."

"Where are you going?"

"I don't know," he said, "but if I stand here any longer I'm pretty sure my heart's gonna explode."

"Okay," Jessie said meekly, watching him walk away down the hall. She shoved the keys into her back pocket as anger suddenly began to rise in the back of her throat. How could he walk out before his daughter's big solo performance, regardless of what Jessie had done to provoke him?

She set her jaw and fought back a couple of tears, knowing she needed to clear her head and get into the dressing room to help Ellie with her costume. The show must go on, as the saying went.

***

ELLIE WAS JUST PERFECT during her solo dance, executing the whole routine with a grace that Jessie was quite sure she herself would never be capable of if she had a million private lessons. She filmed the whole thing with the junky camera on her phone while a mixture of anger and guilt ate at her stomach. Steve had petulantly stormed out of the building rather than staying to watch his daughter dance, but Jessie was the reason he missed it. At least he could watch this grainy version of Ellie's solo when things settled down.

Jessie was grateful when Ellie wanted to sit at the back of the auditorium with her friends from the beginner ballet class – eager to get accolades from them for her solo – because it meant she wouldn't have to explain Steve's absence just yet. She found a seat by herself a few rows away, where she could keep an eye on Ellie chattering with her classmates, and Jessie had no idea whether to cry or be angry as she watched the rest of the dancers perform their routines without really seeing them.

She didn't see Melody again for the rest of the night, and that was probably for the best. The moment her hands had landed on Melody's hips it was like she turned into a teenager again, unable to control her impulses.

When the recital ended, Jessie collected Ellie and they headed for the parking lot.

"Where's daddy?" Ellie asked with a frown.

"He had to leave," Jessie said. She'd spent most of the recital trying to decide how she would explain that she was responsible for Steve missing Ellie's big moment on stage, and she still hadn't come up with anything halfway sufficient. In the end, she did the only thing she could think of – she lied. It wasn't right, but she'd done a lot of things wrong tonight. What was one more? "I'm sorry, bug, but daddy had a work emergency. He saw you dance, though, and he said he's really proud of you, Ellie."

"Oh," she said, frowning as Jessie helped her into her booster seat in Steve's truck. "Okay."

"You know what would be fun?" Jessie asked as she climbed into the driver's seat, trying to make her voice as convincing as possible. "A sleepover at grandma's house! I filmed your solo dance and I bet she'd love to see it."

Jessie had no idea where Steve had gone without the truck or his house keys, and she didn't know if he'd come home tonight, but if he did there was a big discussion looming for them, and it was one that she didn't want to have in whispered tones to keep Ellie from hearing them fight.

"Okay," Ellie said with a sigh.

She was a smart kid and she might not know what was going on between her parents, but she knew enough to realize that the sleepover wasn't up for debate. Jessie glanced over at her, heart breaking as she saw how dejected Ellie looked. She was still wearing her solo costume, but all of the excitement she had on their way to the high school was gone now. Jessie had robbed Ellie of something tonight and she vowed to make it up to her, one way or another.

She dropped Ellie off at her mother's house, pulling her aside to explain that she needed to talk privately with Steve and then taking a few minutes to show her Ellie's dance. That livened her up a bit, and when Jessie left she was performing the routine in grandma's living room.

Jessie was exhausted by the time she pulled into her driveway and she would have liked nothing more than to go to bed and forget all of it until morning. The light was on in the living room, though, and Steve must have used the spare key hidden under the welcome mat. She sighed as she put her hand on the door knob, all of the fight going out of her, but they had to have this talk tonight. It was now or never.

She found Steve sitting at the kitchen table, two empty beer cans crumpled in front of him and another one in his hand. She dropped his keyring on the table and said, "I wish you didn't leave before Ellie's solo."

"I wish you didn't spend the last five years lying to me," Steve spat back. "Do you have any idea how it feels to be the fucking idiot who has no idea his wife is a lesbian, working my ass off to keep us afloat, meanwhile you're out there just having a good old time with that girl in front of everyone?"

"Fuck you," Jessie said, her voice seething. She thought she was more tired than angry and she could count on one hand the number of times she and Steve had lost their temper with each other, but suddenly blood was boiling into her face. "I've never been anything but faithful to you."

"Bullshit," Steve grumbled into his beer can.

"You're not the only one working their ass off around here," Jessie said, and now she was spitting mad. Being polite and working through things like the adults they always pretended to be had gotten them where they were now, so maybe it wasn't so great. It felt good to finally yell. "Everything I've done in the past five years has been for Ellie and you know that. Melody is Ellie's teacher and that's *all.*"

"Bullshit," Steve said louder, putting the can down hard on the table. Little droplets of beer flew out of it and he growled at Jessie, "Maybe you're not fucking her, but you know she's more than just Ellie's teacher. Jess, I know what it looks like when two people have feelings for each other and what I saw in that hallway was a hell of a lot more than a parent-teacher relationship."

"Then why didn't you say something sooner?" Jessie screamed. It felt like every repressed emotion and unspoken word from the last five years was fighting its way to the surface all at once, and if she didn't let it out she might explode. Suddenly her legs were giving out and she slid to the floor against the kitchen cabinets, tears streaming down her face. The salt got in her mouth as she sobbed. "If you know so well what it looks like to be in love then why the hell did you marry me?"

"You were pregnant!" Steve said, throwing his hands up in exasperation. "What was I supposed to do, read your mind? How could I possibly have predicted all of this?"

Jessie put her head in her hands, unable to stop the flow of tears from her eyes. They wetted her palms and streaked her face, and she would have given anything in that moment to go back to the comfortable numbness she had been cultivating so successfully before she met Melody and everything got turned upside down.

Steve let her cry for a minute, and when he spoke again his voice was softer. He asked, "So are you..."

He trailed off and Jessie looked up at him. He looked about as lost as she felt and she already regretted yelling at him.

He sighed and tried again. "Are you a lesbian?"

"Yeah," she said, and a strange smile came to her lips before she could tell herself that it was bad form to be grinning in this particular moment. She'd never said it out loud before – she barely even thought it because she was married and there was no point. But now that it was out there, she realized how right it felt. She held her head a little higher and said, "I'm a lesbian."

Steve looked at her with the same expression of help-lessness that she'd worn the day she took that pregnancy test with Blaire by her side. She'd had to live with that feeling for five long years, and now apparently it was Steve's turn to take it for a spin.

"I don't understand," he said after a moment of contemplation. "You agreed to go out with me. We had fun."

"I went because Blaire asked me to," Jessie said with a sigh. "I went for her. Steve, I've always liked you. You're a good guy and a wonderful father. But I never liked you that way. I'm sorry."

She winced as she said this last part. It seemed so harsh, especially after five years of marriage. She studied Steve's face for signs of pain, but was surprised not to find any. It had all washed away, and a little smile played in the corner of his mouth instead.

"What?" she asked.

He let out a guffaw that echoed through the kitchen, tears coming out of the corners of his eyes. Then he said, "And here I was thinking that you find me revolting on a spiritual level. Turns out it's just that I have a dick!"

Jessie wasn't quite sure how to take this outburst, but she laughed a little. She looked at her husband with sympathy and said, "Yeah, in a nutshell."

"Hoo boy," he said, still roaring with laughter, "I bet you *really* hate those."

Jessie couldn't help but laugh at that one, and when they got it all out of their systems, Steve got up from the table and came over to Jessie. He slid down to the floor beside her and she asked quietly, "So what do we do now?"

Steve took her hand in his in a gesture that neither of them had bothered with since the early years of their marriage, when they were still invested in trying to be a normal couple. He squeezed her hand and said, "Look at me, Jess."

She did, and he sighed.

"I felt so confused and betrayed when I found that lesbian book on your phone," he said. Jessie opened her mouth to respond, but he went on. "And it hurt like hell when I saw you with Ellie's teacher today. When I left the school I just started walking and I didn't know where I was going, but after a while I realized I was walking home. That's when it dawned on me that the thing that hurt most was the fact that you and I are never going to have the kind of connection I saw between you and that girl tonight. I've known that for a long time and I just didn't want to admit it. We're just not meant to be married, Jess."

"What are you saying?" Jessie asked quietly. Her heart was pounding and she was squeezing Steve's hand, afraid of what would come next. This was the moment she had been running from ever since she saw Melody for the first time and knew that her feelings could be dangerous.

"We're a great team when it comes to Ellie," he said. "When I was sixteen, I never thought I'd be happy living hand to mouth like this and working in that damn factory for the rest of my life, but I'd do it all over again for Ellie. You and I have worked like hell to give her a better life than either of us could have given her on our own. But Jess, you have to admit we are a terrible couple."

"So what do we do?"

"Stand up," Steve said, getting off the floor with a little bit of effort and holding his hand out to Jessie.

"Why?"

"Just do it," he said, pulling her to her feet. Then he sank down on one knee and she gave him a funny look. He held her hand and looked up at her. "Jessie Cartwright, will you divorce me?"

"Stop it," she said, rolling her eyes.

Steve got to his feet. "I'm serious. We've wasted a lot of time being unhappy together. Let's be divorced and happy. If we did this good a job raising Ellie while we were miserable, I'm sure we can figure out a way to do it separate but united."

"Okay," Jessie said, taking the cheap silver band off her finger and handing it to Steve. Of all the teen pregnancies and subsequent shotgun weddings in the world, she lucked out when she got stuck with Steve.

CHAPTER TWENTY-FOUR

JESSIE

Jessie's first date was with Steve Cartwright. She'd seen him around school – Lisbon High wasn't a big place and everyone knew each other at least by sight – but he was one grade ahead of her so they never had a class together and she'd never spoken to him. She was going on this date as a favor to Blaire and her heart was pounding as she got dressed and then paced around her living room waiting to be picked up.

Blaire was obsessed with the idea of a double date. She and Josh had been going steady for six months and she wasn't interested in hanging out with Jessie alone anymore. She needed another couple to do stuff with and the idea was that Steve would become Jessie's boyfriend. He was Josh's friend from the football team and Jessie figured agreeing to this date was as good a way as any to spend a little more time with her best friend.

She'd barely seen Blaire since she started dating Josh,

and as it turned out, she didn't see a whole lot of her on their double date, either.

The four of them went to a diner in town and Blaire spent most of the meal absorbed in Josh, kissing him and giggling and generally making Jessie feel like puking. She tried to talk to Steve, but it took about ten minutes before she realized there was no chemistry between them. Certainly not like Blaire and Josh had – they couldn't keep their hands off each other.

So Jessie and Steve ate in silence and Jessie spent most of the meal wishing the boys would just disappear. She wanted her best friend back, and she found herself wishing she could take Josh's place. It would be three more months before she figured out what that really meant.

When dinner was over, Steve graciously paid for Jessie's meal despite the fact that he'd been dragged on this date just like her, and then Blaire suggested they all go back to her house. Her parents were out of town and she had a fire pit in the back yard. She said they'd sit around the fire and have a few beers from her dad's fridge in the garage. That sounded casual and Jessie figured there would be less pressure to act romantic when they were just sitting around talking.

She was wrong about that.

No sooner had Josh gotten the fire started than Blaire was taking him by the hand and leading him into the house. Jessie felt anxious – she didn't want to be alone out there with Steve, struggling to come up with conversation topics. She caught Blaire's eye and tried to convey her panic. This whole thing was supposed to be a double date, and she was beginning to doubt Blaire knew the meaning of that phrase.

Blaire raised her eyebrows at Jessie, nodding at Steve in an expression that clearly meant *go for it*. Just before Blaire and Josh disappeared into the house, she mouthed the words 'spare bedroom' to Jessie.

Then it was just the two of them, Jessie and Steve sitting uncomfortably next to each other and staring at the fire. She tried to count the seconds that they were alone, wondering how long it would be until Blaire and Josh returned. Were they even planning on it, or was Jessie on her own out here? Eventually, Jessie gave up waiting and decided that if she just acted like a normal teenage girl, she might start to feel like one, too. It was impossible to tell how much time lapsed between the moment Blaire disappeared and the one in which Jessie turned to Steve and said, "Do you want to go inside with me?"

CHAPTER TWENTY-FIVE

JESSIE

Steve slept on the couch the night of Ellie's recital and the next morning he and Jessie sat down at the kitchen table again to figure out how to move forward. It felt surreal – they didn't argue any more, and there were no more tears. They calmly discussed the terms of their divorce, and after a few minutes Jessie got up and made Steve a plate of eggs and sausage just like she always did on mornings when they were both at home.

The only difference was that this morning, Jessie woke up with the feeling of a great weight being lifted off her chest. She never noticed it when they were married, but she'd spent the last five years carrying a huge burden like a boulder depressing her lungs and keeping her from taking a full breath. It was gone now, chased away while she slept, and she wanted to fling open every window in the house and take big, gulping breaths of fresh air.

By the time breakfast was over, Jessie and Steve had

decided on a few things – first and foremost that Ellie would always be their number one priority.

"It breaks my heart to think about her not seeing you every day," Jessie said.

"I know," Steve said. "But it's not like I got to see her much during the week anyway thanks to my work schedule. She's already used to seeing me only on the weekends. That's how most people do split custody, right?"

"I think so," Jessie said. There hadn't been much to mourn about the end of a passionless marriage, but she couldn't get over the idea of tearing Ellie away from her father. That had been the whole point of staying with Steve. She stared out the window for a minute, pondering as her eye caught the 'For Rent' sign that never seemed to leave the yard. Then she said, "What if we don't do it like that, though?"

"What do you have in mind?"

"Move in next door," Jessie said, pointing to the wall they shared with the other half of the duplex. "It's for rent. Ellie could go back and forth whenever she wants. It would be exactly like how we are now, except with an extra wall between us. We can have our separate lives and Ellie still gets both of her parents."

"That's not a bad idea," Steve said. "But..."

"What?"

"How the hell could we afford it?" He asked. "We're barely making ends meet as it is, and you want to add a second rent payment?"

"We'd have two rent checks no matter what if one of us moved out," Jessie said. "You know there have been a million different tenants in that apartment since we moved here. I bet the landlord would be thrilled to rent it to trustworthy people he already knows, and maybe he'd even give us a little discount for renting out both halves. Come on, Steve. You know this is a good idea."

IT TOOK the two of them a couple of months to save up the money for a deposit on the other half of the duplex, during which time Steve continued to sleep on the couch. They explained the situation to Ellie as best they could, and after they reassured her that daddy was only going next door and he'd still tuck her in at night, she warmed to the idea.

It helped soften the blow when they told her she'd be getting a second bedroom in the new apartment. It turned out to be a blessing that Mary Beth's was closed for the summer because Jessie could put her whole paycheck toward furnishing the second apartment, and when she realized she had an extra hundred dollars, she decided to surprise Ellie by turning her new bedroom into a dance studio. Jessie bought a dozen full-length mirrors and hung them on one wall, then Steve made a ballet barre out of a handrail he picked up at the hardware store. It wasn't the most glamorous ballet studio in the world, but Ellie flipped when she saw it and Jessie knew that they'd made the right choice renting the other half of the duplex.

The strangest part of splitting up with Steve was

being alone in the bed every night. Jessie had gotten used to the rhythmic, slightly nasal inhale and exhale of Steve's breath as she fell asleep beside him. Now the bed felt huge and empty and she found herself staring at the ceiling for a lot longer than it used to take to fall asleep.

Usually, she spent that time thinking about Melody, and that was strange too – strange in a wonderful way – because it was the first time in Jessie's life when she could think about another girl without an undercurrent of guilt.

Jessie quickly found herself actively trying to fend off sleep just to spend more time with the Melody that resided in her mind. She went back again and again to the way it felt to slide her hand into Melody's, and the way her hips felt against Jessie's palms the last time she saw her. She imagined those stunning chestnut eyes and she craved the chance to act on that desire. The summer seemed to stretch on forever and Jessie thought again and again about the next moment she'd see Melody when dance lessons resumed in the fall.

CHAPTER TWENTY-SIX

MELODY

Melody spent her first summer back in Lisbon hiding from the world in Andy's smoke-filled basement. She thought she'd be doing the same this summer, but a lot changed during the year and she was finding life underground to be less and less appealing. For the first time in almost two years, she wasn't in the mood to hide anymore.

When she came home on the night of the recital, Melody felt a new sense of pride swelling in her chest. She'd stood in the wings and watched Ellie's solo performance, miming the choreography and watching in awe as Ellie nailed the whole thing. When it was over, Ellie ran off stage and threw her arms around Melody, pleased as punch with herself, and Melody cheered her on as she dashed out of the wings to get accolades from her parents.

That was the moment Melody understood what Mary Beth had been trying to do when she forced Melody into the studio against her will. Watching Ellie take the lessons she'd given her and turn them into something beautiful, Melody suddenly felt like she'd found a new way to do ballet – one that didn't involve panic attacks and bleeding toes and inferiority complexes and massive amounts of debt.

The morning after the recital, Melody got out her laptop and started researching colleges in the area. She had enough of performing arts degrees, but she thought she could manage one in dance education.

"I think that's a really good fit for you," Dr. Riley said when Melody brought up the idea.

"I figured I could start in the fall and ask Mary Beth to give me some more classes as a substitute when her regular teachers call off," Melody said.

"Sounds like you've thought a lot about this," Dr. Riley said.

"I guess so," Melody said. "I have a few other things I'm trying *not* to think about."

"Such as?"

"Jessie." She said it merely as a statement, not intending to discuss the matter, but Dr. Riley let the room fall silent so long that Melody started squirming in her seat and felt obligated to explain. "The last time I saw her was at the recital. We had a really intense moment followed by a really awful one. Her husband was there and I think they got in a fight because of me. I keep thinking the worst case scenario is that she doesn't even enroll Ellie for the fall – maybe they go to some other dance studio next year and I never see either of them again."

"Why do you think that possibility bothers you so much?" Dr. Riley asked.

"Ellie was my first student," Melody said, willfully ignoring the thought of never seeing Jessie again. That idea was just too painful to acknowledge, particularly if it turned out to be Melody's fault for giving her husband the wrong idea. "She was my first student and I kinda want to see that through."

"Do you think there's anything to be done about that situation over the summer?" Dr. Riley asked.

"No," Melody said. "Not really."

Even if she had a way to contact Jessie and apologize, doing so would only make things worse.

"Let's put a pin in that one until the fall, then, and see how it goes," Dr. Riley said. This was incredibly unhelpful, but she was right – there was nothing to do until classes resumed. Dr. Riley asked, "So have you told your parents about your idea of going back to school?"

"Hell no," Melody said with a laugh. "Do you know how much they'd badger me about it? I won't tell them until I get an acceptance letter and a financial aid package."

"So you've definitely decided to apply."

"Yeah," Melody said, considering. "I suppose I have."

ON HER WAY home from her therapy session, Melody paused on the sidewalk in front of Andy's lawn. It had been mowed recently – a rare sight – and she suddenly realized it had been a while since the last time she saw him. Her trips down to the basement had been a daily occurrence through most of last year, and as she got busy at Mary Beth's, they started to become less frequent without either of them noticing. Melody cut carefully across the grass and knocked on the door to the basement.

"Who is it?" Andy shouted from the couch.

"It's the golden child," she called back and he yelled for her to come in.

"What the hell's wrong with you?" he asked as she came down the stairs. "You never knock."

"I don't know," she said. "I haven't seen you in a while. Thought maybe you died and your parents hired a landscaper."

"Har har har," Andy said with a roll of his eyes.

"Seriously, have you seen the lawn?" Melody quipped. "It doesn't look like crop circles, but I'm not ruling out alien interference."

"I did it, jerk," he said as she sat down in the recliner. "I started doing some lawn mowing, you know, for a little extra weed money."

He added this caveat in the same way Melody had tempered her parents' excitement when she told them she landed the receptionist job last year, lest they be too proud of her. She grinned at Andy.

"What?"

"You got a job," she cooed. "Look at you, all grown up and responsible."

"Shut up," he said, nodding at the bong in its customary place on the coffee table. "Wanna smoke?"

"Nah," she said, and then because she couldn't help pestering him, she said, "You know lawn mowing is a gateway job. Next thing you know you're going to be sitting at a desk and wearing a tie."

"Never," he said. "They're not even paying me above the table."

"Well, baby steps," Melody said with a laugh. "You want to hear something even crazier? I think I'm going back to school."

"Back to New York?"

"Hell no," she said. "Granville State maybe, or Westbrook. I'm thinking about getting a dance education degree."

Andy took this news without much reaction, saying flatly, "That is crazy. It's cool, though."

It meant that their friendship had just about run its course. They'd both known, at least on a subconscious level, that it had an expiration date and now that they didn't have apathy and weed in common anymore, they didn't need each other. Melody barely missed this basement, with its persistent old sock smell and dank air, but she was happy to see that Andy was moving on as well, even if he didn't want to admit it.

"Yeah," she said. "I think it will be. Well, I just dropped by to make sure you didn't sink so far into that couch that you got trapped or something. Talk to you later?"

"Yeah, sure," Andy said. Melody climbed back up the creaking stairs and when she got to the door he called, "Nice knowing you, golden child."

Then he reached for the bong and she walked carefully across his neatly manicured lawn to her parents' house.

MELODY'S first day back at Mary Beth's in late August just so happened to be a Tuesday morning private lesson. She'd been surprised when Mary Beth called to tell her Jessie and Ellie wanted to continue them, but she had no idea what to expect from Jessie.

Ellie was six now, old enough and dedicated enough to memorize her own routines, so maybe Jessie wouldn't even come inside. Or maybe she'd pull Melody aside to yell at her for putting her in such a compromising position with her husband. Or worse, maybe she'd come in and find a spot along the wall and not even acknowledge Melody.

When the morning came, Melody got up and put on a black leotard with a pleated bust that used to be her favorite back in her Pavlova days. She didn't have much to show off – she'd always been built like a bean pole – but it accentuated what little curves she had and she couldn't help reaching for it when she thought about the possibility of seeing Jessie. She wouldn't mind teasing her just a little bit – in case Jessie planned to ignore Melody through the whole lesson, she would at least make it difficult.

She pulled on the fuzzy pink sweater that she wore during Ellie's private lessons last year, not worried so much as she had been in the past about the possibility of the sleeves riding up. She had a gnarly scar on her forearm, but eventually it would fade and in the meantime, she could finally look at it and see a battle wound instead of an admission of failure. She didn't fail – she survived.

Melody arrived at Mary Beth's a few minutes early, unlocking the door and heading into the studio. She went to the center of the room to do a few warm-up stretches and work through the routine she had already begun to choreograph for Ellie's recital dance this year. She turned on some music and for a few minutes it was just her and the mirrors, enjoying the ballet like she always used to before New York.

Then she heard a familiar shriek behind her. "Miss Melody!"

Ellie dashed into the room, wearing a brand new pink leotard and looking about half a foot taller than the last time Melody had seen her. She held a new pair of ballet slippers in her hands, dangling them by the elastics, and Melody guessed she had probably grown out of her shoes from last year, or else worn them out practicing. Melody used to wear through a pair every six months or so because she danced so much and it was clear that, schedule or not, Ellie was going to be the same way.

"Hey, Ellie," she answered cheerily. "How was your summer?"

She was watching the studio door out of the corner of her eye, waiting to find out if Jessie was here, too, and trying not to get her hopes up too high. Fortunately, Ellie didn't seem to notice her distraction.

"It was good," she said. "I have my own ballet studio now!"

"Oh wow," Melody said. "How'd you get so lucky?"

"My dad moved to-"

"That's enough," a familiar velvety voice scolded. "Remember what we talked about, Ellie."

Melody turned to see Jessie coming through the studio door and tried not to grin like an idiot. She missed the hell out of Jessie, and relief washed over her knowing that their interaction at the recital hadn't been the end of them.

"Sorry," Ellie answered, chastised, and she went to the opposite end of the room to use a chair as she put on her ballet slippers.

Jessie walked further into the room, and Melody's heart almost stopped as she realized Jessie was making a bee line for her.

"Hi," she said breathily as Jessie stopped right in front of her. They were standing far closer than was polite and Melody felt an electric tingle running through her body as she looked into Jessie's moss-green eyes.

"Did you have a good summer?" Jessie asked, and it was such a mundane question it drove Melody crazy.

She didn't want to talk about her summer, and in this moment she didn't want to teach ballet, either. She wanted to push Jessie up against the nearest wall and finally take what she'd been waiting for — that kiss that had been interrupted so many times before. She thought she'd go insane if she had to wait any longer, but she looked over to where Ellie was busy tightening the strings on her slippers, oblivious to the tension building between them. Of course she'd have to wait.

"It was alright. Nothing much to report," she said. She would have liked to come up with something witty to say, but staring into those green eyes so close to her own, she found herself tongue-tied. Eventually, because she couldn't bear not to ask, she managed, "Is everything okay? After the recital-"

"Everything's... good," Jessie said. "Steve and I separated."

"Oh," Melody said, not sure how to react. Jessie didn't look too torn up about it, but it seemed callous to celebrate something like that. Melody asked, "Was it because I..."

She trailed off, not sure how to ask whether her presence at the recital and Steve's reaction to her had contributed to the end of Jessie's marriage, but thankfully Jessie let her off the hook.

"No," she said abruptly, but then a second or two later she added, "and kind of yes."

"Oh," Melody said again. There didn't seem to be much else to say.

"I'm ready," Ellie said, and that's when Melody noticed she'd come to the center of the room and was already sitting on the floor, ready to stretch.

"I should start class," Melody said apologetically to Jessie, who headed for the last chair in the row and pulled out her trusty notebook. Melody went over to the stereo and queued the warm-up music to begin the lesson. Better late than never.

She glanced over at Jessie again and she looked almost embarrassed. There was a lot of color in her cheeks and she was looking at Melody through her eyelashes, her head tilted down toward her notebook. It stirred something in Melody, but whatever that look meant, it would have to wait until the lesson ended.

Melody spent most of the hour reviewing things she'd taught Ellie last year, and Ellie followed right along not missing a beat. It was pretty clear that her new home studio must have gotten an awful lot of use over the summer and Melody thought it would be worth reminding Ellie of the practice schedule that they'd come up with in the spring. Still, Melody couldn't deny Ellie's impressive aptitude for ballet. She even taught her the first part of her new routine before the hour was up.

When the lesson ended, Ellie dashed out of the room to change into her school clothes and Melody found herself alone in the studio with Jessie once again. She didn't know how to proceed or what to say about Jessie's divorce and her part in it – the smart thing to do, as Ellie's teacher, would be to go out to the reception desk and sit down as if Jessie was any other dance mom.

Be professional, she told herself.

But Jessie *wasn't* just another dance mom, and she never would be. Melody walked over to her, heart pounding and totally unsure of what she'd say when she got to her.

CHAPTER TWENTY-SEVEN

JESSIE

Melody was coming toward Jessie and this was the moment she had been waiting for ever since she and Steve separated and he gave her permission to follow her heart. She wanted Melody – she'd *always* wanted Melody – and she stood up. The moment their eyes locked, it felt like all the oxygen had been sucked out of the room. Jessie couldn't catch her breath and she felt blood rushing to her head.

Melody stopped in front of her, so close she could feel Melody's breath on her neck. Jessie licked her bottom lip, catching it briefly between her teeth, and couldn't find enough air in her lungs to speak.

"So," Melody said. "You're single now. How does that feel?"

Jessie couldn't stop falling into those gorgeous chestnut eyes and suddenly she was feeling very clammy and flushed. There were so many things she wanted to say, things she'd rehearsed while she was staring up at the ceiling night after night this summer, but now that the time had come she had no words. She realized with horror that she'd never in her life tried to flirt with someone she was actually interested in and she had absolutely no game at all.

"It's strange," she managed to say. That wasn't sexy. "Steve's living in the other half of our duplex and Ellie's adjusting better than I hoped."

Shit, neither was that. Jessie knew she should be telling Melody how liberating it felt to finally stop living a lie, or even more to the point, how much she'd wanted Melody since the moment she saw her. Instead, this stream of mundane babble kept falling from her lips and she could only watch in horror as she sabotaged her first real chance with Melody.

"I don't think she fully understands what it means yet, but the studio we built for her has gone a long way toward making it okay," Jessie said. She could have smacked herself in the forehead right then and there, but at least she had enough restraint to wait until she was alone to do that.

"She's a lucky girl," Melody said, a shade of disappointment in her voice.

It was so much harder to be smooth and seductive when she had the real-life version of Melody in front of her – in Jessie's fantasies, it had always been effortless. But time had run out and Ellie was standing in the door of the studio, impatiently waiting for Jessie to drop her off for her second day of first grade.

Jessie glanced at Melody, trying not to betray too

much of the disappointment she felt in her expression. All she could do was try again next time, and maybe work on growing a metaphorical pair in the meantime. "See you on Saturday? Ellie's in the morning intermediate ballet class this year."

"Yeah," Melody said. "I'll be here."

Jessie headed for the door, throwing an arm around Ellie's shoulder. She didn't look back at Melody, too disappointed in herself to give her another glance. Because she'd chickened out, she now had another week of unbearable tension to look forward to before she'd see Melody again.

When they got to the parking lot, Jessie was surprised to find Steve's truck parked in front of the school. Jessie furrowed her brow as the driver door opened and Ellie dashed across the parking lot to greet her father.

"Hey, bug," he said, scooping her up and carrying her around the front of the truck. "How was your lesson?"

"Good!" Ellie said emphatically. "Are you going to take me to school?"

"Yeah, if it's okay with mommy," he said, glancing at Jessie. She was too surprised at this unexpected appearance to do anything but nod in agreement. Sure, that was fine, but why? Steve carried Ellie around to the passenger side of his truck, saying to her, "I miss my little bug in the mornings, so I thought I'd surprise you. We can get McDonald's breakfast on the way."

After he got Ellie buckled into the truck, a task made more difficult after he riled her up with the promise of greasy breakfast sandwiches, Steve shut the door and came around the front again to meet Jessie.

She folded her arms critically and asked, "You got up early and came all the way over here to drive Ellie two miles over to the school because you missed her? You'll see her this afternoon."

"That's not the only reason," he said. "Did you do it?"

"Do what?"

"Did you ask her out?"

"You came here to pester me about *that*?" Jessie asked, raising her voice in incredulity.

Steve just smirked at her. "I knew you'd chicken out."

"Jerk."

"No," he corrected. "Wingman. I'll take Ellie to school, you go back in there and ask her the hell out."

Jessie sighed heavily and kept her arms crossed protectively in front of her chest. Why did it feel like she was being coerced?

"Come on, Jess," Steve said. "It's okay to move on with your life. Unless, of course, you want to waste another five years."

"What if she doesn't want me?" Jessie asked.

That was a doubt that had been floating, not yet fully formed, in the back of her mind for a while now. Jessie had never asked anyone out before, and she'd only ever been on a single date. What if she sucked at it, or Melody thought all the fun was in the fact that they were on opposite sides of the reception desk this whole time? It was a lot to put on the line.

"You'll never know if you don't try," Steve said. "Now get in there."

Jessie watched as he climbed into the truck and Ellie waved goodbye to her, and then it was just her, standing alone in the parking lot. Adrenaline coursed through her veins and she made a mental note to do her best to return this favor when Steve started dating and needed a wingman of his own.

CHAPTER TWENTY-EIGHT

Melody leaned against the studio wall the moment Jessie and Ellie walked out of the lobby and she heard the door shut behind them. She let out a big breath, putting her head back against the wall, and she wondered if she should have handled that situation differently.

She shouldn't have left it up to Jessie. She shouldn't have let her turn the conversation into something that any dance mom would have with her kid's instructor. She should have grabbed Jessie and pulled her into the kiss she'd been waiting so long for. Now that the husband was out of the picture, there was no reason not to, nothing holding them back. But when Jessie started talking about her new living arrangements and Ellie's dance studio, doubt set in. Melody started to wonder if she'd made the whole thing up – all the tense moments that passed between them in the last year – or maybe Jessie moved on over the summer and she already had someone new.

Melody shut her eyes and tried not to think about the possibility that she'd fucked things up between them forever by not just going for it a long time ago. She should have kissed Jessie outside the high school last spring and got it over with.

But she didn't want to 'get over with' anything involving Jessie. She wanted to savor their first kiss, especially after she'd spent so much time yearning for it. Who knew if she'd ever get the chance now?

She was so absorbed in this wallowing line of thought that she didn't even hear the front door opening. By the time Melody heard shoes clipping briskly across the wood studio floor and opened her eyes, Jessie was already halfway to her.

"What are you-" Melody began to ask, but that was all she got out before Jessie put her hands on either side of Melody's face and pulled her into a long overdue kiss.

Their bodies came together against the wall and it felt like a static shock, every bit of the tension that had been building between them releasing all at once. It was heaven. Melody put her hands on Jessie's hips and kept her close while she parted Jessie's lips with her tongue and tasted her sweetness. Even if she should have done it a year ago, this moment was well worth the wait.

After a long moment in which she lost track of everything beyond Jessie's lips, Melody pulled back just a few inches – just far enough away to speak – and asked, "Why are you here? Doesn't Ellie need to get to school?"

"Steve took her," Jessie said, her voice breathless and her

body still seeking Melody. Her hips connected with Melody's, pressing urgently against her and making it hard to focus on her words. Jessie ran her fingers through the loose tendrils of Melody's hair and added, "I had to come back and do what I should have had the guts to do a long time ago."

"Kiss me?"

"Okay," Jessie said, laying another long and passionate kiss on Melody's lips. Then she pulled back and said, "But that's not what I meant. I wanted to ask you out. I was so scared that you'd say no, or that you were only interested in flirting with me, or that I've been reading everything wrong for the past year and this whole thing has just been in my head-"

Melody smiled and put her finger over Jessie's lips to cut off the anxious flow of words. She liked the way Jessie's soft lips felt against her fingertip, and the sensation was awakening a new level of desire in her. But she had to wait a little bit longer and get through this moment.

"Ask me," she whispered, taking her finger away from Jessie's lips and trailing it softly over her jaw and neck to rest on the top of her chest.

"Melody," Jessie said, her velvety voice filling the small space between them in the most intimate way. Melody could feel the words coming out of her chest, vibrating against Melody's hand, and she looked deep into Jessie's brilliant green eyes. Jessie said, "Would you like to go on a date with me?"

"I'd love to," Melody whispered, sliding her hand

farther down Jessie's chest. She could feel her heart beating fast. "When?"

"This weekend?" Jessie asked tentatively. "Friday night?"

Melody slid her knee between Jessie's thighs and pulled her closer to her. She brought her lips close to the plump lobe of her ear and she asked, "How about right now?"

"I was picturing a nice restaurant," Jessie said as Melody's hand closed around Jessie's breast and an involuntary moan escaped her mouth.

It was close to Melody's ear, sending a chill through her body. She brought her lips down to the curve of Jessie's neck, tasting the sweetness of her skin and enjoying the way Jessie's body reacted to her kisses. Jessie opened her mouth, struggling to form words as Melody nibbled and kissed her way up to her jaw.

"You know," she said. "Flowers... candlelight... romance... oh hell."

She put her hands over Melody's on her breasts and gave her a look that begged her to continue touching her. Melody grinned at her, taking this cue and wrapping her arms around Jessie's waist. Flowers and candlelight and romance were nice, but after so many months of craving her, they could wait another day or two. This couldn't wait.

Melody pushed them both away from the wall, and then she brought her lips down to Jessie's skin, cradling her head as she kissed her collar bone, her neck, her jaw.

Jessie let out a plaintive moan as Melody's lips worked her way back down her neck.

Jessie threaded her fingers through Melody's hair and pulled her gently back up to face her. The tension returned, hovering between them for just a moment as Melody bit her lower lip and then leaned in again to kiss her. She stroked Jessie's cheek with her thumb, Jessie's breath catching in her throat, and just as their lips met, Melody's hand brushed over Jessie's thigh. It sent a jolt of electricity through them both and Jessie pulled back for a moment to smile at her, a little laugh escaping her lips.

"What?" Melody whispered.

"I never thought this moment would actually come," Jessie said, and then she threw her arms over Melody's shoulders and pulled her into the center of the studio. She kissed Melody again and pulled her down to the floor, their lips never parting and their kisses becoming more passionate and frantic the more places Melody put her hands on Jessie's body. Soon they were stripping each other naked.

Melody yanked Jessie's shirt over her head and found her nipples hard from the cool air of the studio. She wanted to take her then and there, but Jessie grabbed the bottom of Melody's warm-up sweater and pulled it over her head. They both paused for a moment as the pink scar running up her forearm was revealed.

"Let's just..." Melody started to say, reaching for her sweater to pull it back on. They could do this half-dressed. But she trailed off as Jessie gently took her wrist.

She turned over Melody's arm to look at the scar.

"What happened to you?" She asked quietly. Her mossy green eyes were inquisitive, not judging like so many Melody had seen before.

She still wanted to pull her sleeves down and cover her arm, but she said, "I fell against a sharp piece of metal while I was at Pavlova. I had the flu and my legs gave out. It's ugly."

She made another grab for the sweater, but Jessie brought Melody's forearm to her lips, kissing it tenderly and looking into Melody's eyes as she said, "Everything about you is beautiful."

"Thank you," Melody said, breathless.

Then she let out a surprised yelp as Jessie pulled her on top of her. They collapsed on the cool wood floor and Melody's lips found Jessie's again. Their kisses became more frantic and Melody pinned Jessie to the floor, hands over her head as she kissed and licked and sucked every inch of her flesh from her jaw to her hips.

Jessie closed her eyes and Melody loved the little whimpers she emitted every time she touched her. Her tongue found the soft curve of Jessie's breast and then the hardness of her nipple, while her hands ran down Jessie's sides and squeezed her hips.

Melody undid the button of Jessie's jeans and yanked them over her hips, all the while Jessie's fingers threaded through Melody's hair, tied up in a bun and getting messier by the second. And then Melody crawled between Jessie's knees, pushing them apart to make room for herself.

Jessie kept both hands on Melody's head and her eyes

closed while Melody found the soft fabric of Jessie's panties with her mouth. She hooked her fingers in the waistband and peeled them down Jessie's legs, then gently kissed the top of her pubic bone, feeling Jessie's thighs quiver and close tighter around her.

Melody opened her mouth, her tongue gliding over the soft skin of Jessie's upper thigh and then the crease of her hip, and just before she found the wetness between her legs, she felt Jessie hooking her hands under her arms and pulling her back up.

"What's wrong?" Melody asked, her fingers still playing around Jessie's hips and tracing their way closer to her inner thighs. Every part of her body was on fire and it didn't seem possible to draw in a full breath, she was aching so fiercely for Jessie.

"Nothing," Jessie said breathlessly. She pulled Melody in for another kiss, their tongues dancing over each other and increasing her desire, and then Jessie said, "I've just never done this before."

"Do you want to stop?" Melody asked, a little crest-fallen. Her fingers hovered over Jessie's hip, barely brushing the skin, and she wanted nothing more than to hear her delicious moans again.

"No," Jessie said breathily, and then she grabbed Melody's hand, plunging it between her thighs.

Melody gasped in surprise, her whole body igniting with arousal at the sudden contact. She felt Jessie's breath against her ear and her own body responded to Jessie's undulations beneath her. She slid her hand in and out of the wetness and a shiver went through her every time she felt Jessie's breath catch, her moans echoing through the empty studio.

Melody felt Jessie's hand on her hip. It slid slowly, tentatively down her thigh and then over her backside. Melody let out a moan to let Jessie know she liked the caress, and Jessie's hands became bolder, grasping and squeezing at Melody's curves. As Melody continued to stroke Jessie and they rolled their tongues together, she felt Jessie's hand slide between her thighs, her fingers moving the fabric of Melody's leotard aside and finding a wetness of her own.

Melody let out a loud moan that resounded through the room and threw her thigh across Jessie's body. Melody could feel her tightening and pulsing around her hand, her thighs clenching and her body reacting to every stroke of her fingers, and she had been waiting for this moment for so long that she knew it wouldn't take much to bring her over the edge. They climaxed together, a knot of flesh and sweat and desire undulating on the floor.

They lay together for a while afterward, catching their breath and enjoying the coolness of the floor against their backs. Jessie threw her arm over Melody's waist, pulling her close, and when Melody turned her head she could see the two of them intertwined in the mirror. She liked what she saw and she thought she'd never mind being in the studio again if she could replace all of those bad New York memories with this one.

"I just thought of something," Melody said after a while, kissing Jessie's forehead.

"What?" Jessie asked, tracing her finger over Melody's stomach and then swiping a sweat-drenched tendril of her dark hair away from her face.

"There's a class here in forty-five minutes," Melody said with a laugh.

"Oh shit," Jessie said.

She practically jumped off of the floor, reaching for Melody's hand and pulling her to her feet. Jessie scrambled to gather her clothes and stepped back into her jeans, but then Melody grabbed her by the hand and pulled her into another lingering kiss.

"It's okay," Melody said as they separated again. "We've got time."

"It's not that," Jessie said with a laugh. "I just realized I was supposed to go work a shift at the grocery store after I dropped Ellie off."

"Shit," Melody agreed, tossing her shirt over to her. "You better go."

Jessie took a few quick strides for the door, pulling on her shirt as she went, and then she turned around and dashed back across the floor to Melody, nearly sliding into her over the waxed hardwood. She asked, "How about three o'clock this afternoon for our date?"

"That's a little early for dinner, don't you think?" Melody asked.

"It is," Jessie said, "but that's when I finish my shift and I don't want to wait a moment longer than I have to. We'll go to dinner, and then if I'm lucky we'll do this again, except maybe with a bed next time."

"It's a date," Melody said, smiling.

Jessie gave Melody a quick peck on the lips, and then she dashed out of the room, leaving Melody to clean up the room and get ready for her receptionist shift to start. She picked her sweater up off the floor, then paused for a second to look at the scar on her arm. It was already beginning to fade. She smiled, put on the sweater, and then waltzed across the studio floor with a big grin on her face.

EPILOGUE

Her first month with Melody had been one of the best of Jessie's life. Every day was like a new experience, and she didn't realize just how numb she had been when she was trapped in a marriage whose only goal had been the care and financial security of her daughter. Looking back, it was easy to see how gray the world had been when she was living a life that wasn't her own. Now, with Melody lending her perspective, it was hard to imagine how Jessie made it five and a half years with nothing to keep her going except Ellie.

The whole world felt different now, brighter. She didn't resent romantic comedies anymore, and she didn't look away when she saw couples kissing in public. They didn't make her uncomfortable or jealous anymore because she finally what it felt like to have that.

It was like a rebirth, and when Jessie came out the other side she realized just how beautiful life could be.

She and Melody went to the same fancy Italian restaurant on their first date that she went to with Steve on their anniversary. If there is been any other halfway decent restaurant in Lisbon, she would have taken Melody someplace different. But as it turned out, the Italian place was a whole new restaurant when she was looking across the table at Melody.

Suddenly the tea candles in the middle of the table made sense and she didn't feel like the only person in the dining room who whose heart was made of stone. She used to keep her head bowed down and her eyes on her plate, but now it seemed absurd to focus on the food when all she wanted to do was reach across the table and take Melody's hand in hers. She wanted to play footsie beneath the table, and kiss her and stare into her eyes, and skip straight to dessert.

On their second date, Jessie let Melody choose their adventure and they went hiking on a trail Jessie didn't even know about not far from Lisbon. Melody packed a picnic and they set out early in the morning before the sun had a chance to fully rise. It was chilly and, admittedly, they didn't do a whole lot of hiking. They ended up sitting on a huge boulder overlooking the town, kissing and talking all morning like silly teenagers until was too cold to sit any longer and their appetites got the best of them.

Jessie never tired of learning all the little things about Melody's life. She opened up to Jessie by degrees, slowly feeding her details about New York and what it was like to be on track to become a professional dancer. She talked about Andy and how she spent almost a year of her life as a deadbeat instead of the dancer she was supposed to be, and what it was like to come back from that failure. She was taking general education classes at the community college until she could enroll in a dance education program, and they were both working on putting their lives back together after a detour. Jessie's was, admittedly, a bit longer than Melody's detour.

One day, Melody came over to Jessie's place after class toting a brochure. She held it up for Jessie to read the cover – a GED program sponsored by the college – and she said, "I think you should do this."

Melody was juggling school and work at Mary Beth's, and Jessie still had two jobs plus Ellie's schedule to work-around. It was hard enough to find little moments during the day to see Melody, and even now Jessie only had about an hour and a half before her next shift.

"How could I add that to my plate right now?" Jessie asked. "I couldn't make it work when Ellie was a baby, and I have way more responsibilities now."

"We'll make it work," Melody said confidently, and when Jessie gave her a look that said she was thoroughly unconvinced, she added, "You gave me hell once upon a time about not being motivated enough to follow my dreams. Well, now I'm supplying *your* motivation."

"When would I even go?" Jessie objected. It wasn't like she never thought about going back to school, but she barely slept as it was. To add night school to the mix seemed like an idea destined to fail.

"That's the beauty of it," Melody said. "The program

is mostly online. I'll loan you my computer if you need one and we can carpool to campus on days when you have tests. Otherwise you just do it whenever you have the time. What do you think?"

"I think you're incredible," Jessie said with a sigh. That plan sounded so achievable, and she didn't want to let herself get too carried away with daydreams of better jobs and more money and nicer hours.

She took Melody's hand and pulled her closer. Ellie was still in school for another hour and Jessie would have to give in to the chaos of her life again then, rushing Ellie across town to her mother's house for the evening while she put in a quick shift at the diner. For now, though, it was just her and Melody. She slid her free hand up Melody's thigh.

Melody raised an eyebrow and said, "Does that mean you'll do it?"

"Just give me the brochure," Jessie said with a wry smile, snatching it out of Melody's hand and tossing it on the table by the door. "Thank you."

"You're welcome," Melody said with a satisfied smirk, and then she gave Jessie a teasing look, biting her lower lip in a way that never failed to drive Jessie up the wall. "Now, how much time did you say you have before work?"

"About ninety minutes," Jessie said, not breaking eye contact with Melody. "Why?"

"That's plenty of time," Melody said with a grin, then she turned and dashed down the hall toward Jessie's bedroom.

Jessie's heart was already racing as she followed her. Melody was making Jessie chase after her like they were a couple of teenagers, and she didn't mind it one bit. It kind of felt like being a teenager again, living a life that was interrupted and which she never thought she would have a chance to replay.

No sooner had Jessie come through the bedroom door than Melody turned and pounced on her, swinging the door shut behind them and pushing Jessie backward toward the bed. She tripped over the corner of the rug and lost her footing, and suddenly she was falling backwards onto the mattress. Melody's eyes went wide, the trip having been unintentional, but when Jessie landed there unscathed she didn't waste any time running after her.

Melody pounced onto the bed, throwing her leg over Jessie's hips and straddling her, covering her in kisses and letting her rich brown hair fall across Jessie's face as she bent over her. Jessie reached up and yanked at Melody's shirt, pulling it over her head and then unhooking her bra. They had been together for such a short time, but Jessie was already starting to know Melody's body. She took her soft breasts in her hands, thumbs rolling over Melody's nipples, and Melody responded by arching her back and moaning into the empty apartment.

"You are so hot," Jessie breathed, her whole body already tingling with desire. Blood was rushing into her head, making her feel euphoric and excited, and the first few times she and Melody made love she'd had to choke back a tear or two. Sex never used to feel like anything special to her, but the moment her body connected with Melody's, everything started to make sense.

The moment Melody's lips first touched Jessie's, color erupted into her world. Her body tingled and her fingertips craved Melody's flesh, and her lips felt at home against Melody's in a way that felt like a light switch turning on in her mind. *This* was what everyone else was going on about when they talked about sex, and romance, and love.

Melody was so right.

"You're irresistible," Melody whispered now, her breasts heaving beneath Jessie's hands as her breathing intensified. Jessie loved the way it felt when Melody's thighs were wrapped around her hips like this - it was a feeling she never wanted to forget. She put her hands on Melody's hips and squeezed, moving her body against Jessie's lap and eliciting a moan from her soft lips that sent another shiver down Jessie's spine.

Melody unbuttoned Jessie's shirt, one of the dingy white dress shirts that she had to wear to every shift at the diner. She draped over the edge of the mattress, careful not to wrinkle it, and then all bets were off. Jessie grabbed Melody and flipped her onto her back, pulling up the teasingly short skirt she was wearing and yanking her panties all the way down to her ankles. Jessie was getting very practiced in the ways that Melody liked to be touched, and knowing that she could elicit any reaction she liked with just a few specific motions turned Jessie on more than anything.

As Jessie slid her hand between her thighs, Melody unbuttoned Jessie's work pants and pulled off her shoes, setting the black pants down in a neat pile on top of her work shirt. Then they were both naked, their limbs entwined.

Jessie stroked her hand over Melody's body, their mouths together as she rolled her tongue over Melody's lips. She moved her thumb in small circles over her, and the way Melody's hips moved and pushed against her thigh, Jessie could feel her getting closer to the edge. Her breathing quickened against Jessie's neck and she threw her hands over her head, squeezing the pillows at the head of the bed in her fists.

Jessie watched Melody snap her eyes shut, a plaintive moan drawing out from her lips that Jessie very much wanted to capture and keep. She lowered her mouth to Melody's and kissed her passionately as her hands moved between her thighs and Melody slowly tipped into her climax, squeezing her legs tightly around Jessie's hand as her body quivered and rocked against her.

When the spasms of her body died down, Melody craned her neck up and gave Jessie a soft kiss, then she pounced again and pinned Jessie's shoulders down to the mattress, her hands lingering on Jessie's biceps as she crawled down to the foot of the bed.

Giving Jessie a seductive grin, Melody grabbed her legs and pulled her to the edge of the mattress, then she looped her arms beneath Jessie's thighs and lowered her head. Jessie put her head back and closed her eyes, and she felt Melody's tongue on her, and her hands squeezing her thighs. Melody licked and lapped at her and Jessie threaded her fingers into Melody's hair, guiding her head where she needed her tongue's attention.

Jessie didn't last long with this motion, feeling herself getting closer and closer to the edge. She raised her hips and squeezed her thighs against Melody's head, craving the release that she was teasing out of her. But she had just enough presence of mind to put off the inevitable for a minute longer, and she grabbed Melody by the hands, pulling her onto the mattress and then throwing her onto her back.

Jessie climbed on top of her and without another moment's hesitation she thrust her fingers between her legs, grinding her hips against Melody's thigh as her hand moved in and out of her, each of them moving against each other in rhythm. Their breaths rose and fell together as they got closer and closer to the edge. Just a few thrusts more and Melody was coming again, her whole body twitching and convulsing around Jessie's hand, and then Jessie felt her hips taking over, grinding out her orgasm before she collapsed next to Melody, gasping into the bedsheets.

"You're getting really good at that," Melody said with a wicked grin, wiping her hair away from her face.

"What can I say? I have a good teacher," Jessie said teasingly.

Melody smiled and tenderly kissed her nose, then glanced over at the alarm clock. It was already ten til three. "Isn't Ellie going to be home soon?"

"Yeah," Jessie said, nuzzling into Melody's neck as she pulled her closer. "Just a few more minutes, please."

Melody threw her arms around Jessie and squeezed her tight, and for the first time in her life, Jessie knew with absolute certainty that she was where she should be.

AUTHOR'S NOTE

Thanks for reading *Falling Gracefully* – I hope you enjoyed it!

If you did, please consider leaving a review on Amazon or Goodreads – they make a big difference in the success of indie authors like me, and they help more readers find awesome LGBT content.

If you'd like to connect with me, stay up to date with my latest writing projects, or just chat about your favorite lesbian fiction, you can find me on Twitter and Facebook @caramalonebooks

You can also read deleted scenes from this book, preview chapters from my works in progress, behind-the-scenes peeks, and occasional notifications about giveaways and events by joining my twice-a-month email list. Go to cara-malonebooks.com and click Newsletter to sign up.

Thanks again for reading, and I hope to hear from you soon!

With love,
Cara

ALSO BY CARA MALONE

When Hannah inherits her Aunt Nora's house unexpectedly, she finds herself completely unprepared to deal with the renovations it needs. Nora's neighbor Avery has the knowledge and patience to help her tackle the project, but before long Hannah realizes that the house isn't the only fixer upper in her life.

Read on for a preview chapter from this book.

ONE

AVERY

A very Blake realized too late that her pickup truck wasn't the best-equipped vehicle to transport little old Nora Grayson. First of all, the cab was about two feet higher than Nora could even lift her own leg at the age of eighty-four. Avery had to take her by the arm to steady her and then more or less heft her into the seat, noting the papery quality of Nora's skin and wondering absently if she could hurt her with this motion.

Secondly, there was no good way to secure Nora's oxygen tank and keep it from flying all over the bench seat, so Avery had to keep one hand on the steering wheel and one on the portable oxygen. This was made all the harder by the fact that Avery hadn't thought to clear out the tools that were always banging around in the foot wells – she really should have planned this outing better, but who plans for a funeral?

She was just thinking that she really should have forked over the cash to have Nora transported in some kind of medical van when they pulled into the driveway of Nora's old house. The trip from the nursing home back to Nora's place – right across the street from Avery's – had been mercifully short, but the journey to the funeral home would be a longer one and Avery wasn't looking forward to juggling the oxygen tank and her octogenarian neighbor – along with her meds and the packrat purse she'd brought along with her – thirty miles down the road.

"We're home," she said to Nora as she threw the truck into park and got out. She walked around to help Nora down, glancing at the house as she went.

It was an old Victorian house with peeling yellow clapboard and lots of ornate details that had been succumbing to dry rot in the years that the house stood empty. Avery spent a lot of time on her porch in the summers, and therefore a lot of time watching the gradual decay of the house. She wasn't sure she wanted to bring Nora here and let her see what had become of it, but Nora insisted. She wanted to find something of Minnie's to remember her by, and Avery knew Nora's good-for-nothing kids wouldn't be bothered to bring her here. They weren't even going to the funeral.

Avery helped Nora down out of the truck cab, leaving the oxygen tank momentarily behind and letting Nora lean heavily on her arm as they made the short walk from the truck to the house.

"It's not very pretty anymore, is it?" Nora asked, sounding a little winded as they reached the top of the three creaky steps onto the porch. "Just like me, old and decrepit."

"Stop," Avery scolded, patting Nora on the back of her hand. "It just needs a little love."

The foyer was dark and Avery could see the dust stirring in the air as they walked in and disturbed it from the floor. It was hard to believe that Nora had only been gone two years – the house felt ancient and forgotten, and even the sheets that had been draped over all the furniture had a thick layer of dust on them.

"Do you know what you're looking for?" Avery asked.

There were a lot of dusty sheets in the living room alone – Nora lived in this house for almost fifty years, first with her husband and then with Minnie, and that was a lot of years to fill a house with the kinds of knickknacks and tchotchkes that she figured Nora would be looking for. The funeral was in two hours, and Avery was starting to wonder if they had enough time for this detour after all.

"I think there's something in our bedroom," Nora said, and her voice was so frail that Avery had no idea how she could possibly make it up the stairs, let alone through the next few hours. Minnie had been everything to her and they spent the last fifteen years inseparable until Nora's kids split them up. Nora made a move for the stairs and Avery took her elbow.

"If you tell me what it is I can go up and get it," she offered.

"Thank you, dear," Nora said, "but I'm afraid I'll only know it when I see it."

"Let me help you up the stairs, then," Avery said, walking beside her as they took them one riser at a time.

It was like climbing Mount Everest and Avery thought that it might be easier to carry Nora on the way back down. She couldn't weigh more than ninety pounds dripping wet. When they finally reached the landing, Nora gestured for Avery to wait for her in the hall.

"Do you want me to hold your bag?" Avery asked, reaching for the purse slung over Nora's shoulder that she hadn't stopped clutching since Avery picked her up from the nursing home.

"No," Nora said quickly, "It's not a burden."

"Okay," Avery said, watching Nora shuffle down the hall to a closed door near the window. "Holler if you need me."

Nora disappeared into her bedroom, the door swinging almost shut behind her, and Avery stood around in the hall. There was an antique oak credenza opposite from the bannister, covered in a thick layer of dust just like everything else, and a mirror that was starting to lose its silver hanging above it.

To kill the time, Avery walked over to it and blew a cloud of dust off the glass, stepping out of the way while it settled. Then she inspected her short, dark blonde hair, normally untamed and falling across her forehead, to make sure it was still neatly slicked back. She straightened the tie around her neck and brushed away the wrinkles that had set into her jacket and pants on the ride over.

NORA WENT INTO HER BEDROOM, putting out her hand to the dresser by the door for support. Walking through the house and seeing everything covered in sheets had been hard enough, but the bed was something different entirely. She walked over to Minnie's side and ran her hand over the blanket, smoothing the wrinkles out.

Minnie always made the bed as soon as they got out of it in the mornings, and turned it down meticulously each night. It even used to irritate Nora the way she tucked the sheets so tightly under the mattress. Nora preferred to give her feet a little more freedom to roam in the night... but what she wouldn't give to feel the tightness of the sheets around her toes now.

A plume of dust rose into the air as she tidied the bed, reminding her that it had been two full years since she last slept in it, and three since she shared it with Minnie.

Nora turned away from the bed before the tears had a chance to come to her eyes. She went back over to the dresser by the door. It was covered in a sheet like most everything else and the top of it was lumpy since whoever closed up the house hadn't taken the time to pack away the knickknacks before covering the furniture. Nora carefully lifted the front of the sheet, more dust flying, and revealed a nicely organized collection of figurines on top of the dresser.

Most of them belonged to Minnie. She started collecting the little ceramic women during the war, while she and Nora were raising their families and their husbands were fighting in the war. They'd been an occasional splurge to balance the pressures of working and homemaking and child rearing.

A few of them belonged to Nora, though. Minnie had gifted them to her at a time when symbolic gestures were all they could share, and they continued to mean a lot to Nora. She wanted to bring them with her to the nursing home, but she couldn't bear to separate them from the rest of the collection.

Now, she picked up a figurine in a full-length pink dress and a bonnet decorated with gold foil accents – a Clarissa – and wrapped it carefully in a kerchief she brought with her. This was the very first figurine Minnie ever gave her, and it always held a special place in Nora's heart. She tucked it into the bottom of her purse, and then with a glance toward the bedroom door, she pulled a small leather journal out of her bag. She tucked it into the top drawer of the dresser, beneath a pile of neatly folded slacks where she hoped no one would bother to look.

Then Nora opened the bedroom door and announced to Avery, "Okay, dear, I'm ready. I appreciate your patience with an old woman."

THE FUNERAL WAS SMALL, primarily populated by Minnie's children and grandchildren. They all thanked Nora for coming out to pay her respects to an old friend, and Avery watched her face carefully for a reaction.

She didn't think she could stand it if she lost someone as close as Minnie had been to Nora and no one even acknowledged her grief, but Nora seemed to take it in stride. They'd hidden their relationship for so many years, Avery figured she was just used to playing the role of the best friend. It was more than Avery would have been able to do.

Nora held it together like a real trooper through the entire church service, watching solemnly as the casket was wheeled down the aisle toward the altar and dabbing delicately at the corner of her eyes while the priest spoke. Avery was standing by with tissues and the oxygen tank and a supportive hand if need be, but Nora turned out to be a lot stronger than she looked.

She didn't really break down until they lowered poor Minnie into the ground.

The cemetery was wet with last night's rain and Nora clung to Avery's arm as they walked to the grave site. She thought it was just that the terrain was rough going and Nora's modest one-inch heels were sinking into the earth with every step, and it wasn't until the priest said his final prayer over the casket that she realized Nora was clinging to her because she might crumble to the ground otherwise.

A small yelp, something like a wounded animal would make, came from Nora's lips while everyone else crossed themselves and muttered an *amen*, and then Avery felt Nora's weight pulling on her arm as her legs went to jelly.

She dropped the oxygen tank to the wet grass and

held onto Nora, keeping her on her feet and pulling her into her chest for support as she sobbed. Most everyone headed back to their cars after the casket was lowered, a few of them looking at Nora with a mixture of pity and confusion, and Avery felt the urge to lash out at them rising up in her throat.

Who the hell were they to stare at her grief?

Move it along, asshole, she wanted to growl when their eyes lingered on Nora, and Avery held her tighter to keep her from the realization that she'd become a spectacle for them.

When they got back to the truck, Avery practically carrying Nora across the grounds, she carefully looped the oxygen cannula over Nora's ears and brought it to her nose. Avery gave her a few minutes to settle down before starting the trek back to the nursing home, and the way Nora's face was twisted into a physical manifestation of the pain of losing Minnie really ate at Avery.

In a million years, she couldn't be as strong as Nora had been in her life, or as tenacious as she'd been in her love for Minnie. And she certainly couldn't face a moment like Nora went through today. If this was the heartache people signed up for when they fell in love, she didn't want any part of it.

Visit www.caramalonebooks.com/books
for a complete list of novels by Cara Malone.

Made in the USA
Middletown, DE
01 September 2018